Les Jeux sont Fate

...and other tales

Peter Gillies

Les Jeux sont Fate

...and other tales

artwork by
Magdalena Adomeit

A·B·C·

abceditions

enjoy life & love others
be you & have fun

A·B·C· EDITIONS • FRANCE

Les Jeux sont Fate ...and other tales
ISBN 978-2-9584200-6-2

• • • • • • • • • •

To my father…

who, typing his letters
on a Smith Corona keyboard,
introduced me to the music
of putting words down on paper

The tales

Les Jeux sont Fate

'AGAIN?'

THE GODS TURNED ON THEIR omnidirectional axis and frowned as one. Would there never be a moment of peace? A lasting lull in which to indulge themselves with untroubled shut-eye? Why did the knockoffs in their image think everything had to lead somewhere? For the love of God – to *be*… simply to be. To dance. Wasn't it enough? The thrill of movement, rising-falling, coming-going, twirling-sailing, dashing-drifting… Surely life's eternal whirl through ever-expanding space should fill them with joy. Just to be – alive, footloose, and fancy-free. Couldn't they get their kicks with that? Why in Heaven's name were they so hung up on love?

'We'll be down in a wink,' they said with one voice.

The messangel withdrew from the celestial presence and returned to the lower spheres from whence she'd come. There was shouting in the wings. It was most undignified.

'Take your pinions off me! I won't, I tell you! I won't! I'm fed up with all the waiting!'

The head of reincarnation went to meet her.

'Will they come?'

'They say they'll be down in a wink.'

'It won't be too soon. This one's a case.'

'Go on, you! Beat it! Leave me alone!'

The burly archangel yawned with pointed disinterest. Let the captive gripe to his heart's content. So far, she hadn't laid the tiniest tip of a feather on him; why bother herself with shutting him up? Foolhardier angels might find him rather cute, all worked up as he was – a quixotic soul astride his high jinx horse. She had better sense: he was wayward and quarrelsome, a recusant rebel with no hope of finding his cause.

There was a knock at the door. The messangel poked her head inside.

'The gods are waiting,' she announced, smiling sweetly.

'Let them wait,' snapped the detainee. 'I'm not leaving here till my demands are met.'

The archangel yawned again.

'Out with you. You can present your case in person. May the gods have mercy.'

Struggle he might, but the soul was no match for the archangel's authoritative will – she plucked him up by the seat of his awareness and unceremoniously steered him to the stoop, where she dropped him in a dishevelled heap at the messangel's feet.

The archangel yawned yet again – 'If you can help it, don't bring this one back; I'm short forty winks' – and with that, she shut the door.

'Listen to her,' snorted the soul, putting himself to rights and dusting off his auras. '*Short forty winks.* Sleep is a fool's paradise.'

The messangel eyed him with a soupçon of impish grin.

'I beg your pardon. Are you suggesting I'm a fool?'

The soul hesitated, but stood his ground.

'I – well, yes. If you're fond of sleep, then yes, I am.'

'I see,' replied the messangel with archly feigned coolness. 'And why, may I ask, is sleep a fool's paradise?'

'I – '

'Is it because fools escape their woes when asleep?'

'I – '

'Is it because fantasies fulfilled in dreams are immaterial and never last?'

'I – '

'Is it because sleep's warm embrace is an ephemeral sham, compared to the abiding rapture of love's Elysian pleasures and cosy cuddles?'

She'd hit the nail on the head three times running. The soul couldn't have said it better.

The messangel chucked him under his chin.

'We'll take the long way. It'll be more fun.'

The gods were waiting, but she knew they wouldn't mind. For the gods, any delay that prolonged the eternal now was a welcome moment to enjoy.

‘Mind you don’t get tangled in the strings.’

The messangel seemed to brush aside what looked like quivering threads as they ambled along. The soul had never been so far off the beaten track. It was all new to him.

‘What if I do?’

‘What?’

‘Get tangled up.’

‘How should I know? You might gum up the works. If you do, it’ll be your own fault.’

‘Oh,’ said the soul, sufficiently awed by his potential for significance that further enquiry was moot. ‘I’ll be careful; but if you ask me, the works are already gummed up.’

The messangel pulled up short.

‘Whatever are you talking about? The entire universe is working just fine. It’s only you who’s got a problem.’

‘Me?’

‘Yes, you. What’s your quibble?’

‘I – ’

The heat of the messangel’s stare was giving him pause. He felt seen. Exposed.

She raised her brows in a call for reply.

‘Love,’ he said at last.

‘What do you mean, love?’

‘I – I want my true love.’

The messangel blinked, as if faintly bemused.

‘Your true love? Is *that* your quibble?’

The soul was serious, dammit. He defended his dignity.

'Yes, that is my quibble. But it's not merely, as you would have it, a quibble. My grievance is of the highest order. I'm fed up with waiting. I've been waiting for eternity.'

'Waiting for what?'

'For what? To *meet* her, of course. I want to meet my true love. And it's got to be her – not some ersatz love. I'm done with this endless merry-go-round – falling in love, again and again, always with the wrong people. I don't want to waste a single lifetime more. I want my true love – now!'

'What's wrong with the wrong people?' asked the messangel, disconcertingly nonchalant.

'What's wrong with... what's wrong with the wrong people? Are you bonkers?' he blurted. 'Don't you know anything? With the wrong person, it's doomed to fail. It doesn't matter how well it starts off; sooner or later, it runs off the rails. And where does that leave you? I'll tell you: in a mire of Boredom. Indifference. Loathing. Hostility. Why, even downright Hatred.'

'Gracious. Sounds grim.'

'It's grim all right. And that's if you're lucky. Love that's not true is a damned rocky road. Boredom and loathing and hatred aren't the half of it. It's awash with infidelity. It's a road so rutted with rutting, so strewn with potholes of promiscuity and boulders of betrayal, that it pummels you with wretchedness and breaks your heart.'

'But – what's wrong with that?'

The soul stared at her. Was she serious?

'You lived through it, didn't you?' said the messangel with a kindly smile. 'And if it breaks your heart, as you put it, then it even does you some good. Besides, it's you who keeps falling in love with the wrong people. You don't have to. You could always fall in love with someone else. There are plenty of lovely people to fall in love with on the merry-go-round, as you call it.'

The soul dug in his heels and stood his ground.

'No. That's not what I want. I don't want just any love. I don't want a slightly better love, or even a good love. I want my true love. My one and only. I want the love of my life, the one who's my other half.'

'Ahh...,' said the messangel, assuming a solicitous gravitas. 'You want your *soul*-mate. Is that it?'

'Yes. I want my soul-mate. That gifted Greek was right. I just know it: she's out there. And I won't rest till I find her.'

❧

'Where is she now?'

The gods were entwined as always, a luminous presence, an evolving steady state of consummating love. Their radiance was unbearably bright. As a rule, they kept themselves under wraps when they were not strictly alone, but for the occasion they'd come down from the ethereal heavens without their veil.

'She arrived on Venus a few winks ago,' said the head of reincarnation, averting her eyes. 'I have to say, we were lucky to get him away in time. It was a close call. He is proving most uncooperative.'

'He won't reincarnate?'

'He will not. He refuses.'

The gods were baffled. They often cursed free will for being a bane and a blight and would have gladly scrapped it altogether, but their hands were stayed by a mighty catch: without it, there wouldn't be a spark of life to nurture and cherish.

'And she?'

'As vivacious as ever,' sighed the head of reincarnation with a smile. 'A peach. She'll happily return at the drop of a hat. She never tires of the fun.'

'Well, at least one of them has some sense,' said the gods. 'Here's what we'll do. Bring her back. The mischief-maker can miss a few turns. We have no truck with lovesick fools. Keep Peaches in play, and we'll send ol' Firebrand back to Venus for another spell. Let him cool his heels and pine away to his heart's content.'

The messangel took in the view. Earth was the prettiest little planet – so vibrant and varied, so boundlessly creative and chromatically adorned. It cradled her most cherished memories. On Earth, she'd loved countless men and women in her time. Incarnating as both in repeated cyclic fashion, she'd explored every nuance of love until she'd received the gift of desire in every conceivable configuration. She smiled at her remembered raptures and sighed to herself. What fun she'd had! It was something to be alive.

Beside her, the soul was fidgeting. He peered into the star-spangled blackness of space stretching in every direction, distant and cold. No doubt there were other worlds out there, far-flung and unexplored. So what? He'd had enough of novelties. What did it matter, how many mountains you climbed or seas you sailed, how many empires you built or quests you conquered? Mountains and seas? Empires and quests? Trifles, mere trinkets – soon stripped of their shine and fast worn thin.

The soul scoffed. No, what mattered was Love. The key to unlocking heaven? Love! The clearest-cut answer to life's Gordian riddle? Love! The sine qua non of empyreal bliss? Yes, Yes, a thousand times Yes – Love! And still, Love was ever so much more than that – infinitely more. What was Love? The aspiration to which all creation purposed. The eternally awaited quintessential union. The apotheosis of a soul's starry hope. For each and every soul there was but one true love, one matchless match, one transcendent pairing – and no two souls could rest until they had each found the other, their heart's truest desire.

'But where would that get you?' asked the messangel softly, divining his thoughts.

The soul considered this with a faraway look in his eyes.

'Home,' he sighed, wistfully savouring the word.

The messangel was touched. They'd discussed his past

lives on their peregrination round the solar system. He wasn't the querulous spoilt child she'd first taken him for. He was sincere. Like her, he'd loved and been loved in every configuration and context. He'd started by only loving the right people; when he'd run through the universe's stock of right people, he'd given loving the wrong people a whirl, intent on leaving no stone unturned lest the jewel he sought was playing diamond in the rough. He'd thrown down the gauntlet in his search for true love… and still he'd come up empty-handed.

By now, thought the messangel, any other soul would have put two and two together. Any other soul, going through what this one had gone through, would have attained a state of enlightenment and happily stepped off the merry-go-round. Why so pertinacious in the face of futility? Why so dogged in fruitless pursuit? Why didn't he wake up? To be an angel was divine. To defer to one's divinity was paradise. To leave one's kismet unfinished, unsettled, unresolved; to step aside with good grace; to forswear attaining one's apogee with a smile and delight instead in being a satellite of the gods' all-embracing dance, content to simply see it continue unabated, forever and for evermore.

'I don't suppose you'd reconsider? Trying to get home, I mean.'

The soul strove to linger a moment longer in his evocative rêverie, but she'd broken the spell. He turned to face her beatific mug and glowered.

'You *are* obtuse, aren't you. I said no – No, No, a thousand times No. I want my true love. I won't settle for less. I'm done with having my heart broken.'

'Ah, yes,' said the messangel, 'your heart. Broken, you say. Do you really think your heart can be broken?'

Was she mocking him? The soul took umbrage. He wished to make his point abundantly clear.

'I know it can. Broken. And not only Broken. Smashed. Smithereened. Shredded. Flayed. Racked and Rent, Bludgeoned and Cudgelled. My heart's been so Pierced by Shards of Hope Dashed it's a wonder it still goes on beating. And you have the nerve to ask me if a heart can be broken? Mine is the living proof.'

'Yet it still goes on beating. It still plays life's happy tune. That doesn't sound like it's broken.'

The soul was vexed by her gentle look and kindly smile.

'Oh, what would you know?'

The messangel gave him another chuck under the chin.

'Don't you see? Your heart has never been broken. What's been broken every time is just a part of a shell you think is there to protect it. Every time that shell of yours takes a hit, gets broken a bit more, its jagged edges cut into your heart. It's painful. I know. But the more that shell gets broken, the more it falls apart, the more shards are cast off – until one lovely day, it's so positively in pieces that it simply crumbles into dust, leaving your heart free. Free, at last – to love, and to be loved, naked and unafraid, in pure and joyous union.'

The soul was exasperated.

'But don't *you* see? All you've just said is all that I want –

only I want to share it, that bliss, with my one true love.'

The Earth kept circling on course in cosmic suspension. Across the orbital plane, forever out of reach in her own elliptical groove, Venus was playing hard to get. The soul's one true love was there, resting her auras for a spell in binary limbo, yearning no less ardently than he, her heavenly match, for that forbidden meeting to occur.

'Do you know what would happen if you did?' asked the messangel thoughtfully, contemplating distant Venus. 'Have you the faintest idea?'

The soul had a dreamy notion.

'The very first time you fell in love,' she went on – 'do you remember how it felt? Or later, when you fell in love anew, hopelessly tumbling head over heels? Or, with your heart broken, as you say, and having sworn off love for good, when you couldn't help falling in love yet again, but this time with someone who was your complete opposite and drove you right round the bend – your heart so full of love, pounding as though it would burst?'

How could he forget? Every new love was like that. Every rush of new adventure was headier than the last.

'But it never lasts,' lamented the soul. 'It never lasts.'

'Of course it never lasts. But do you remember how it *feels*?' insisted the messangel. 'That's what I'm asking you.'

Yes, he remembered – his auras, undulating with elation… his breast, heaving with heart-thumping desire… his days, fired with such immediacy that life itself thrummed with excitement. Propelled by passion to until-then-unsuspected heights, he would glimpse dizzying new vistas of happiness he'd feel sure were within reach. To consummate such love was to embrace the holiest of holies, to find oneself clasped in a beatitude that, if only for an instant, suspended all space and time. There was nothing to compare. They never lasted, but those moments, stolen from eternity, were a timeless joy.

'Well, if you ever met your soul-mate,' said the messangel, pointedly interposing, 'that moment would be so many zillions upon zillions of times more ardent still that you've simply no clue what you'd be letting yourself in for' – *or anyone else*, she added to herself, knowing full well the effects of the singularity that would occur. No, it was simply too stupendous, too fraught with irreversible ramifications. The cosmos from start to finish would be consumed in the flash.

'My advice: don't go there. Better love in small doses. Satiety in small feasts. Many small sweet drops of nectar, spread out over lifetimes, are more safely enjoyed than a sweeping deluge of rapture unleashed in one go.'

The soul was torn.

'Besides,' the messangel went on, conspiratorially lowering her voice, 'the truth is – although I shouldn't be telling you this – the gods have ordained that such meetings must never occur.'

'What?'

The messangel nodded knowingly.

'It's the foundational Law of the Universe – the law upon which the sacred perenniality of the gods' happily-ever-after hinges,' she explained. 'Overstep that bar, and the universe to an atom is instantaneously wiped out, its cosmic bubble burst by the cataclysmic trysting of two meant-to-be's.'

'Do you mean to say I'll *never* meet my true love? Never ever?'

'Yup. 'Fraid so,' said the messangel. 'Never ever.'

The soul was incensed. Confound it! The whole game was rigged, the outcome foregone. A fate, no less, ordained by the gods – the selfish rogues! They only cared for their own abiding happiness. All this time, he'd foolishly hoped there was a chance for his own. But no… and never ever, at that!

The messangel, regarding him with compassion, smiled to herself. He was cute, but he was a slow learner. Still trapped in desire. Still intent on grabbing a gold ring. He wasn't yet done with the merry-go-round. Poor soul – until he realised that his fixation on love was the wellspring of all his unhappiness, he'd keep on going in superfluous circles.

The soul shook his head, palpably disheartened.

'Well… what are my options? You may as well tell me.'

'Your options? Rather few, I'm afraid. You can return to limbo on Venus – '

The soul immediately recoiled at the thought. All those god-forsaken, love-sick souls, milling about in half-hearted circles, retailing ad nauseam to whomever would listen their hackneyed tales of love come to nought. He hated Venus.

' – or you can go along with the gods' plan, which has you going back to Earth again.'

'That's rather futile, isn't it? I mean, if there's no chance in heaven I'll meet my true love?'

'Being alive is never futile. It's very nearly the best thing going.'

He gave her a questioning look.

'What's the best?'

The messangel only smiled. That, one had to find out for oneself.

A fine wink's work, thought the messangel on her way to report to the gods. *And won't they be pleased, not having to deal with the matter.* Oh, the poor soul had grumbled a bit, but he'd let her coax him into giving it another go.

'That's a good sport! This time, you'll love it. You'll see. In no time you'll be over the moon and on your way. She's just over there – see?'

They'd watched with quiet elation as the moon had drawn near, gliding along on her orbital round, majestic and proud, brightly bathed in sunlight… a precious jewel floating in space, a soul's stepping stone for returning to Earth. The moon, the moon! Did lovers know, why she captured their fancy so? Could they divine in her shadows each day's fill of souls, queued and primed – keen to carpe diem as lovers entwined, to quicken life sparked by their carnal embrace? Ah, Love! It truly did make the world go round. The imperishable desire to unite drove the universe's unceasing movement; it was the fuel that fired its everlasting evolution, the power that wrought miracles. Without love, the world would be but a static continuum of humdrum inertia; *with* love, it was sure that its freewheeling, ever-changing, exhilarating dance of life would go on forever.

'Now, cheer up,' she'd said, playfully chucking him one last time under his chin. 'Who knows who you'll meet? Who you'll love, and who will love you? It'll be fun either way. Put aside your chagrins, and let me see you smile.'

The soul had reconciled himself to his fate. He'd thought he'd be too glum to smile, but the tingling prospect of loving once again had its charms. He was feeling optimistic.

'It's still a sham,' he'd demurred. 'But I'll admit that you're right about one thing: until something better comes along, Life is the best thing going.'

'That's the spirit! Now, look. Here comes the moon. You can climb aboard as she passes and join the others in the reincarnation queue. Fair enough? No hard feelings?'

'No. No hard feelings. By the way, thank you for taking me under your wing. You've been very kind.'

'It's been my pleasure. Here she comes, now. No looking back, and remember – enjoy yourself!'

And with that, the messangel had given him a friendly nudge in the right direction.

The gods were melding in their tight embrace, oblivious to distraction. Theirs was a fusion in perpetual bliss, timeless in every moment.

There was a knock on the firmament.

'Be admitted,' they returned – 'and no peeking.'

The head of reincarnation alighted in their presence, taking care to blinker her gaze with tips of her wings.

'Be welcome,' said the gods charitably. 'What news do you bring?'

'I have just come from the moon. I have left the peach there. She is all aflutter with happy anticipation, awaiting her moment in concert with the others.'

'Then all is well. Now we need only await our messangel's return. Where do you suppose she is, anyway? Entangled in the strings? That wouldn't be like her.'

'I cannot account for her whereabouts. Is there anything else you wish me to do?'

'No. Nothing more need be done. But do let us hope things stay calm for a while. We're all in need of catching up on our winks. You may go.'

The head of reincarnation withdrew, the firmament closing behind her as she left.

The gods were pleased. The peach was poised to reincarnate. They'd soon send the firebrand packing. That was how you maintained order in the universe: you nipped rebellions in the bud. The whole crazy dance could carry on without end so long as blunders were averted. Vigilance was the key. The slightest failure to forestall unforeseeable trouble risked sparking repercussions of incomputable proportions.

There was another knock on the firmament.

'Be admitted,' returned the gods with cheery expectancy.

The messangel fluttered in and gracefully touched down. The gods started, thunderstruck.

'Where's the soul-mate?' they exclaimed as one, stupefied to see the messangel standing before them alone. She was beaming.

Wide-eyed, the gods blinked.

Once.

The next instant, there segued an all-consuming,

all-renewing,

all-dazzling

FLASH

Jack o'Lantern

LONG AGO, IN THE ROLLING HILLS of farmland that lay like a blanket across the land, there once lived a good, honest farmer named Jack. A faithful husband to his wife, the queen of his heart, and a devoted father to his daughter, the apple of his eye, Jack was a hardworking soul with a lively spirit and a quick wit, who liked prankish fun almost as much as a second helping of warm pumpkin pie. He was also a bit of a night owl. When the moon shone bright, anyone peeking out their bedroom window in the wee hours might see him slipping past his front gate, heading off down the road for a long, nocturnal ramble with nary a care for spirits or shadows. Something about the night enchanted Jack. The woods were full of life, and he loved to hear the hooting queries of owls, the rooty snuffles of hedgehogs and badgers, and especially in autumn the rustling of fallen leaves underfoot as he strode along the country byways in his old worn boots.

Of course, there was always the chance that Jack might meet up with a ghost out there in the dark. His neighbours often warned him about that. In those parts, all a careless fellow had to do was kick up a clod of earth or pull a stick out of the ground, and lo and behold, a dead man's ghost might follow. You could never be sure where the danger might lie. For centuries, wars and brigands had wrought their handiwork throughout the land, snuffing out mortal lives well before their time. Hastily buried in shallow, makeshift graves, those victims from the past could hardly rest in peace – and they waited on tenterhooks for a chance to spring forth and reclaim what had been snatched from them so unjustly. Disturbing a dead man's ad interim abode put a living man at dire risk. In a trice, the freed spirit would rise up and surely steal off with that living man's mortal claim to life, usurping his soul's place and leaving the hapless fool to wander disembodied and dispirited till the end of time.

Even so, this could never happen during the day, when the sun's life-giving light protected the world of the quick from that of the dead. Any apparitions out haunting the night were sure to dissipate with the sun's first rays, dissolving like the morning mists and returning to their graves. But when the world retreated once again into darkness, then the dead had their chance and the tables could be turned. Farmers knew they ran no risk ploughing their fields by day; yet as the sun sank low in the west, woe to the man who tarried. Better to be safely home with one's horse in the barn, than to be waylaid after sundown by a ghost you'd inadvertently ploughed loose.

Certainly, no man with his wits about him would ever be

so foolish as to work his fields after dark. Stories were told of imprudent farmers who'd pressed their luck, trying to plough one last row. If their husbands were late getting home, wives were never sure if the man who finally walked in through the door were the same husband they'd seen off that morning. Sometimes, an inexplicable change would overcome a man. All of sudden, from one day to the next, he'd be different. Then a wife would be on her guard, until she could decide if she liked this new man or not. Happily, such changes weren't always for the worse. Some wives who were especially unhappy with their spouses even took to locking their husbands out of the house at night, in hopes that a ghost might take his place and bring some happiness back into the marriage.

Jack's wife, though, loved him as he was, and it's sure she would never have wished to trade him for a long-dead ghost, however gallant or good-natured. On mornings when she discovered he'd been out for yet another night-time stroll, she would scold him for his recklessness and beg him to stay in bed with her at night, where it was safe. But Jack would only laugh.

'Don't you worry, my sweet little wife,' he would coo. 'No ghost's going to get the better of me.'

Any night he'd been out for a wander, Jack would quite naturally sleep through most of the following morning before he finally woke. Instead of breakfast, he'd come downstairs to the midday meal, and only set off for his fields in the early afternoon. Once he got going, though, he farmed as well as the rest. Even better. His fields produced the finest corn, his orchards blessed him with fruit in abundance, and the vegetables he tended in a patch out back of the house were the envy of his neighbours. Even if he did get a late start to the day, you couldn't fault Jack for being lazy. He enjoyed working the land, and his wife and daughter never wanted for anything.

So it was, one late autumn day – with the sun already well past its zenith and his best field still awaiting his attention – that Jack donned his broad-brimmed hat, hitched up his horse and went off down the road. Along the way, he waved to his neighbours who were all hard at work carving long straight furrows. That year the harvests had been gathered in, thankfully enough, before an unseasonable spell of rain had kept everyone at home for several idle weeks. But when clear skies returned at last, and with the fields in need of ploughing and winter soon to bring frost and snow, the farmers all hastened to make up for lost time by working long, hard days, until diligence paid off and they saw their work nearly done. Most of his fellow farmers would soon be stabling their horses. They warned Jack that the fleeting Indian summer wouldn't postpone winter indefinitely.

As Jack walked his horse along the road, he was invigorated by the crisp autumn air. The swirling yellow and orange and red leaves falling from the trees gladdened his heart. At last he came to his favourite field. It was the largest he had, a choice bit of land that sloped gently from the road down to a stand of willows that formed its lowest border. Whistling to his horse, Jack set his plough to work turning the rich earth, back and forth. He counted the field as taking a good half a day to plough; still, if the earth yielded easily and his horse worked well, he could usually do it in less. Today, though, the ploughshare struggled to carve the furrows; it snagged on rootlets and ploughed up stones. Jack had to stop twice to sharpen the blade. The sun journeyed ever westward and finally the shadows grew long.

'Hey ho!' called a neighbour from the road. 'Let's be going home, Jack. It'll soon be sundown.'

'Later, Tom,' he answered with a wave, hardly pausing. 'I'll be doing another row first.'

'Don't be foolhardy. You and I both know you won't finish that field today.'

But Jack kept his plough to the task and just waved again. His fellow farmer shook his head. It was no use warning Jack. Some men were just plain stubborn.

A little while later, another man from the village passed by on his way home. He too urged Jack to join him on the road. The dull ruddy disc of a full moon was rising in the east, and the sun was fast disappearing below the horizon.

'Best be getting home, neighbour,' he advised. 'We're late as it is. No use our getting caught out here after dark.'

'Oh, it won't be dark tonight,' replied Jack with a jovial nod to the east. 'I've asked my friend there to come help me make up for lost time.'

The solicitous farmer shrugged his shoulders and walked on. Some men were born fools.

Jack wasn't feeling the least bit tired, and he gauged he had only a wee hour's worth of ploughing left. The field would then be ready for its winter rest, and tomorrow he could tend to his two other fields, which were smaller and situated on the other side of the village. He'd lose a whole day if he had to come all the way out here again just to furrow a few final rows.

Turning his horse round, Jack paused for a moment to admire the beauty of the moon, now white and full and cresting the trees that lined the road. He flicked the reins and pushed the ploughshare into the dirt as his horse started forward. Together they furrowed another row, clear across the field, and then patiently turned back and did the same in the other direction. Corn roots and stones were overturned with the crumbling clods of dirt, but nary a spirit jumped free. His father and grandfather had ploughed this field for so many years before him that Jack reckoned there wasn't a ghost of a chance of finding a spectre still lurking in the soil. The evening grew chilly, and the horse's nostrils blew misty white wraiths. Jack fetched his coat from where it hung on a willow branch.

'Just a few more rows, old friend,' murmured Jack, patting his horse's flank. 'I don't know about you, but I rather like having the moon for company. One doesn't suffer the heat of day nor the glare of the sun. I dare say we should do this more often.'

Soon, the field was nearly finished, and Jack was smiling with satisfaction as he followed his horse down the very last row. His thoughts were turning to hearth and home when, lo and behold, the ploughshare struck a deep rock and dislodged it, inadvertently rending the hallowed stillness of a long-dead man's unmarked grave. Exhaling a spectral hiss, the buried spirit broke free of its earthly prison, rising up before Jack like a nebulous cloud of vapour until it stood wholly formed as the man it used to be.

'Great Scot!' chortled the ghost with glee. 'That's a right fine turn you've done me.'

Jack pulled the reins with a start. The horse paid the ghost no mind, because the horse had no opinion of ghosts, but Jack stood rooted to the spot. Here was the last thing he'd expected to see, all the more so since he had never seen one. 'Twas strange how deathly pale the figure appeared. You could see there was nothing there, and yet you saw every feature as if in half-light. The phantom wore clothes tailored in a style that had long since gone out of fashion, and the waistcoat bore a dark stain where a dagger must have dealt a fatal blow. A ruggedly handsome face, set off with long sideburns, suggested he'd been a man with a keen zest for life, till bad luck had led him to travel by this road where evildoers had robbed him of his future, setting upon him with murderous intent and disposing of his corpse in a roughly dug grave down by the willows. It was an untimely death that a misguided ploughshare had now freed him to avenge.

Even so, Jack didn't quake. Doffing his hat, he steadied his nerves and spoke up.

'Well, sir, you've certainly given me a scare. I guess I never thought I'd run foul of a ghost.'

'No, we're never prepared for our life's worst turns,' concurred the apparition, passing a few ashen fingers over his waistcoat. 'But when they come, so they be, and that, as they say, is that.'

A philosophical phantom. Not a bad sort. Jack wondered if the ghost had any human feelings to which he could appeal. He certainly had nothing to lose in trying.

'I say, sir, you do surely speak the truth. What's fair is fair in life and in death, and with that I won't quibble; for your standing there now, I've no one to blame but myself. So it be. And so I know it is your right, as befits the custom, to depose my soul and take its place before this night ends. But before you do, I wonder if I might seek your indulgence for a trifling favour.'

The ghost stretched his spectral limbs. Oh, to live once again, in this glorious world! To hear children laugh, to watch the seasons pass. To feel a woman's lips upon one's own, the caress of a hand. Oh, to romp with abandon! He wondered if the farmer's wife were a pretty lass.

'Ask, and we shall see.'

'Well, sir, as I say, I don't deny you've every right to claim my mortal place. To your spirit I gladly yield, all the more so since you've waited so long, as anyone can see. But you know what it is to bid life farewell, and for me it will be until the end of God's days. I do so love my little wife and my daughter. Could you spare me one hour, good sir, so that I may hasten home one last time and bid them both farewell?'

The ghost considered this. A poor mortal man's last wish. To live one hour more. As a man, the ghost had been both gallant and good-natured. Death had not changed him.

'I will grant you the time for one last kiss,' vouchsafed the ghost. 'When the village bells toll the midnight hour, I will come for you.'

'Oh, I do thank you, sir,' said Jack with heartfelt relief, respectfully bowing his head in gratitude. 'I will wait for you then. You will find me at my house, first on the left as you enter the village. I'll be sitting on the porch in my old wicker chair. I won't try to hide.'

'It wouldn't matter,' observed the ghost. 'I will find the flicker of your spirit wherever it might be. When next I see the light of your soul, I will take my rightful place.'

Jack wasted no time unhitching the plough. Swinging himself up to ride bareback, he snapped the reins and shouted *Giddy-up!* His startled horse leapt forward, breaking into a canter across the field.

'Faster, faster!' exclaimed Jack, holding onto his hat and urging his horse to a gallop. 'We've no time to spare!' They raced down the tree-lined road through a jagged pattern of tangled shadows and broken moonbeams.

The village was deserted and deathly quiet. By the light of a solitary candle, Jack's poor wife was sitting at their parlour window, keeping an anxious vigil for her husband's return and fearing the worst. Her neighbours had said they'd seen him at dusk, still ploughing his field like a stubborn mule and heedless of their warnings. The approaching sound of galloping hooves broke in on her anguished thoughts. She looked to the road and saw Jack and his horse turn past the fence and rush headlong towards the barn. Her enduring apprehension and sudden joy had hardly had time to untangle themselves when Jack burst in through the back door moments later. He threw a great heap of straw on the floor.

'Hurry, my little wife,' cried Jack, with a mischievous twinkle in his eye. 'A ghost will be your husband in the morn if we're not quick. Fetch me a sturdy knife.' Kissing her brow, he slapped her fanny and rushed back outside, calling over his shoulder, 'A knife!'

A ghost! Jack's wife nearly fainted. She ran to the kitchen to fetch her best boning knife.

Having raided his vegetable patch, Jack soon returned carrying a rotund orange pumpkin.

'Look lively, my lovely bride! We haven't much time.' He set the pumpkin on the floor at her feet. 'Carve open the top round the stem and scoop out the seeds. I've always promised you no ghost would get the better of me, and tonight I mean to keep my promise.'

As his wife got busy with the pumpkin, Jack stripped off his boots and clothes. He fell to his knees and set to work, stuffing his pants and shirt with fistfuls of straw. When the garments were packed full enough to hold their shape, he carried them out to the porch and seated them in the wicker chair, which he backed against the wall by the parlour's broad windowsill. In the shadows, anyone would guess it was Jack sitting there in his day clothes and boots, but he still needed a head. Jack hurried back inside the house.

'Here, now. Pass me that knife. 'Tis a pity to sacrifice such a fine pumpkin as this to save my soul. I would have liked him better in one of your pies.'

Jack worked deftly. In the side of the pumpkin, he carved two holes for eyes. He then fashioned a nose with two curling nostrils, and a wide, grinning, toothy mouth.

'There's your good husband. Handsome fellow, isn't he! Now let's bring him to life.'

Fetching the squat holder from the sideboard, Jack set the lit candle inside the hollowed pumpkin and closed it with the cap. He carried the glowing lantern outside and set it jauntily on the windowsill, on a level with the shoulders of his straw likeness.

'That should do it,' he reckoned, placing his broad-brimmed hat on top of the pumpkin head. Just then, the clapper set to striking the bell in the village steeple.

'Good luck to you now, old fellow,' whispered Jack, half to himself, half to the pumpkin. He rushed back inside the dark house and silently pressed the door shut.

As the bells tolled on – *bong, bong, bong* – Jack and his trembling wife, cowering at the parlour window, fixed their eyes on the road. They soon saw the ghost. He was coming towards the village, floating like a trail of smoke, wending and weaving with a gossamer gait. But his course was not aimless. Without pause, he turned when he came to the first house on the left and advanced towards the front porch with purpose. There he could see the poor mortal man seated in his wicker chair, the flickering light of his soul bright with life. Oh, to live once again! His time had come at last, and he would defer it no longer. Life! Just as the final stroke resounded from the steeple bell, the ghost dove in through his victim's eyes with an urgent rush and fused himself irrevocably to the brilliant dancing light, investing it with his spirit.

But, what was this? He found himself clinging to a candle-wick. Where was he? To what anatomy was he wedded? He sought to raise an arm or lift a leg or turn his head, yet no limbs obeyed, no muscles responded. And what eyeholes were these? He looked through them and was astounded to see Jack.

'How do you like that?' chuckled Jack, standing in his drawers on the porch before the straw man with the carved pumpkin head.

'You've tricked me!' cried the ghost.

'Ho, ho! Tricked you? Yes, I guess I have. And a good thing, too. You see, my pretty little wife likes me the way I am. She didn't fancy the switch you had in mind. Oh, oh! Steady now,' advised Jack, 'or you'll blow yourself right out.'

The ghost's rage was making the candle flicker wildly.

'It's not fair! I've a right to take your place. You know that!'

'Yes, you had the right to take my place,' admitted Jack – 'but you chose to quicken the candle instead. Can I help it if you mistook its merry light for my own?'

Had he usurped Jack's spirit and slipped into his mortal skin, human death alone would have had the power to sever the bond. Now he would survive for only as long as the wick had wax to draw; from the looks of the stumpy tallow, he wouldn't last the night. The ghost struggled to free himself, but he was stuck fast to the tremulous flame.

'Assassin,' hissed the ghost, the candle spitting and spluttering with his indignation. 'You're no better than the men who slew me by the road.'

'Tut-tut,' scolded Jack. 'Call me an assassin if I snuff the candle.'

The ghost was aghast.

'You wouldn't!'

Jack left him in doubt and went back inside the house. He and his wife sat by the parlour window, whispering as they kept an eye on the pumpkin head's orange glow.

The poor ghost was trapped, his fate sealed. Darkness was going to take him once again. Oh, cruel trick! Had he taken Jack's place, he would have had to die again anyway, but even so – at least he would have loved, laughed, lived for a while longer than this. He'd been robbed of his life. Not once, but twice. What a mockery of his hopes, to be taken in by a grinning pumpkin lantern',s dancing candle. He flickered wanly. The liquid pool of tallow grew shallow. The wick drooped and curled, and when a piece broke off and fell, there was too little left to sustain the light. The brilliance dimmed. Then, with a sudden, mute valediction, the flame simply vanished and gave up the ghost.

The following day, Jack's miraculous escape was the talk of the town. His neighbours, rightly astonished, all agreed that his clever trick had worked like a charm. Word spread. Farmers in other villages were keen to learn how Jack – 'with nothing but an ol' lantern' – had saved himself from the spectre's fearful clutches. No wonder, then, that it soon became common practice throughout the land to carve pumpkin lanterns in the fall, when farmers ploughing their fields ran the greatest risk of finding themselves pursued by ghosts. This is why, even today, we find lit Jack-o'-lanterns standing sentry at night on front porches everywhere, ready to hoodwink any ghosts who might be stalking our mortal souls.

And in the end, Jack got to enjoy a pie made from his fine pumpkin after all, for as his good little wife and daughter both said,

"Twould be such a shame to let him go to waste…'

The man of God

'ME! BARRED from Heaven! Why, that's preposterous. Do you even know who I am? This is outrageous. A man of my calibre? Held up at the turnstile like a common sinner? Unheard of! I demand an audience with God. He'll sort this out. You'll see!'

Saint Peter rattled his keys. The righteous were a bane.

'An audience with God is out of the question,' replied the saint with calm certitude. 'I already know his thoughts. God himself instructed me on your case when we heard you were on your way up.'

'Good Lord, man! What *are* you blathering about? Know His Thoughts. Ha! You're raving. What possessed Jesus to sign you as a disciple, anyway? You sot. The Gospels imply *he* drank a lot, but *you* must've been a tankard!'

Some polite coughing in the queue reminded the saint of his duties.

'Yes. Well. Be that as it may, your name, as I've said, is not recorded in our Book of Life. So... I cannot let you pass.

Sorry about that. Better luck next time, as we say around here. Tongue in cheek, of course. Would you be so kind? Please do step aside. *Next!*'

'Now just you wait one moment, Saint Peter. I will not step aside! *You've* made a hash of things. That's perfectly clear.'

With unflinching clarity, the Keeper of the Keys fixed the man before him. Since time immemorial, not a day on Earth had gone by without men of such bent scourging and martyring innocent souls. Verily, verily, men of God were a plague. Without compunction, without mercy, without a scintilla of humility in their hearts, they dared to judge others according to what THEY deemed to be God's word. Zealous defenders of dubiously dubbed 'sacred' scriptures, they high-handedly imposed their self-approving interpretations of sin and duty on all whom they could sway, unleashing fire and brimstone, imprisonment and torture, stonings and beheadings, defenestratious executions and inquisitional autos-da-fé... all in the holy name of God. It was a travesty that made the high-and-mighty Almighty bristle with rage. 'How dare they! In *my* name, no less! Just wait 'til they see what I've got in store for them,' he'd thunder.

With a discreet nod, Saint Peter signalled to a winged attendant, a burly power who'd learned his trade in the streets of Babylon, back in the day.

'... Why, I'll have you know I've had men of your ilk horsewhipped for bungling the dictates of God's Holy Will. You cannot fool me. I know the Mind of the Creator better than anyone. He rejoices in those who defend His Pure Purpose.

He exalts those who punish sinners with His unyielding Judgement. He reserves Heaven's highest honours for paragons like myself who, knowing and prizing His Law, take it upon themselves to… hey! Take your hands off me!'

A brief scuffle ensued. The man of God, however, was no match for the power, who quickly had him clapped in chains and – taking hold of his Achilles heels – at his mercy.

'You ham-fisted flunkey! You've no right! I command you to desist! This is scandalous. What kind of an operation are you running here? You're behaving like demons!'

The power, dragging his charge to the lifts, turned a deaf ear to the vociferous diatribe that seethed in his wake, venting spleen and spraying spittle to the four winds.

'You'll burn in Hell for this, Saint Peter! No one bullies a man of God with impunity! I have friends in the highest places! I'll see you hanged, drawn, and quartered! You'll eat your own innards, choke on your chyme! I'll treat you to torments ghastly beyond measure!'

The doors to the lift opened. The power hauled his charge to his feet and pushed him inside.

'Mark my words, you fraudulent saint! You won't get rid of me like this! I'll petition God personally! So help me, I'll make you rue the day I came knocking on *your* gate! You'll forfeit every last favour God ever…'

The doors closed. Save for a sigh of relief that rose from the queue, a blessed silence enveloped the Pearly Gates.

Peter pressed God.

'You're quite sure?'

'Absolutely. He outclasses them all. Has there ever been a man of God more wicked, more egregiously iniquitous? I know this is all my fault to begin with, but still...'

A pregnant silence succeeded the ellipsis. Too principled to contradict God's word, Saint Peter left the Almighty to stew in the Truth.

God's topmost-level decision to bypass the usual provision for atonement and instead send this one straight down to Hell was unprecedented. As a rule, blameworthy souls were always parked in Purgatory, God's playground for penitents. Heartfelt expiations were both hard-won and rare, but it was nevertheless felt that even the most odious offenders should be accorded the benefit of the doubt. 'I am, after all, a merciful god,' intoned the Almighty dryly. But his rule was unsparing: men of God either wised up and purged themselves of righteousness, or he'd bar them from Heaven indefinitely. 'No exceptions. And I don't care how long they wait,' he added, insouciant about the ranks of recalcitrant heel-coolers swelling with every passing century. 'So long as I'm in charge, no one gets in who thinks he deserves it.'

But when news arrived that the most hateful man of God of all time had breathed his last and was on his way up, the One True God threw his mighty forbearance to the wind.

'I won't have it! He's incorrigible. For the love of all that is holy and good, I refuse to accord him the slightest mercy. Make a note of that. No second chances. He's the worst of them all and a discredit to Creation. Why, he's capable of poisoning all of Purgatory with his bilious preaching. Bar the way. Keep him out. Send him forthwith to Hell, and let Satan do what she will. I wash my hands.'

The power and his onus were seated in a pleasant chamber, ensconced in softly padded armchairs; a delicate scent pervaded the room, wafting from a sideboard where lay a freshly-picked bouquet; a portrait of a regally winsome woman with sparkling eyes hung on the wall opposite. The man of God twiddled his thumbs. He studied the image with feigned disinterest. The woman was stark naked. She was also appealing. *Very* appealing. Tempting indeed. Did they think he was the sort of man who'd trade his Heavenly Reward for the favours of a hussy? Ha! The joke was on them.

He cast a sideways glance at the power.

'Are we here to test my mettle? I can stand up to anything, you know.'

The power seemed to consider this. He held up one finger.

'Fool! Think again. Men of God are made of sterner stuff. I could resist the lascivious lures of a thousand hussies.'

The power shook his head. He braced himself. He'd heard footsteps approaching and muffled voices in the corridor.

'What is it *this* time?' huffed Satan, barging into the room on the heels of an acolyte who had briskly opened the door. 'Can't you people manage up there on your own?'

The power had already stood up and was willing himself not to lay eyes on her too closely. The last time, he'd fallen so far under the spell of her unconcealed charms that he'd nearly switched camps.

The man of God, meanwhile, frozen in his seat, had instantly recognized the woman in the portrait – and was himself caught so far off guard by her nudity in the flesh that he appeared petrified.

Satan looked down at the man in the armchair. His unblinking eyes seemed frightfully close to bursting.

'Oh, *Lord*,' she blurted. 'Is *this* your problem?'

The power applied himself to maintaining an air of dignity as Satan began hooting and howling. Even the acolyte, though mindful of her duty to project decorous gravitas, couldn't help but titter. It was all too comical. Exasperated by their deplorable disrespect for his person, the man of God struggled to his feet with a furious scowl and a mighty rattling of chains. He was determined to meet this horrid gorgon head on.

'You abominable woman,' he bellowed. 'How dare you come before me unclothed! Do you know who I am?'

At this, Satan shrieked with abandon. Her guffaws went ricocheting down the hall.

The man of God turned to the power.

'Where on Earth have you brought me? I won't stand for being ridiculed like this, not by her, not by anyone! Who is this woman? It's not *me* whom you should clap in chains – it's her! She's a disgrace! I've never been so affronted in my life. And by a naked *woman*,' he spat with disgust – adding, 'She's obviously in the power of Satan!'

The mirth unleashed by this unwitting remark was too much. Satan's paroxysms redoubled, the acolyte capitulated to an avalanche of giggles, and even the power was helpless to resist: collapsing in his chair in a humour-stricken heap, his face streamed with tears. The last time, he'd been plagued by a spate of seminal dreams. This time, he painfully surmised as convulsions split his sides, his ribs would be aching for a fortnight to come.

'No, no, and no. You know he's not our problem. He's yours, through and through – and you know very well why.'

Saint Peter had cringed when he'd caught sight of her. Up she'd marched to the Pearly Gates with the man of God still bound in chains and the power, gingerly limping, in tow.

'Yes. Well. Be that as it may,' ventured the saint, nervously rattling his keys, 'his name, as I've said, is not recorded in our Book of Life. So… I cannot let him pass.'

Those waiting in line were as patient as lambs. The advent of the queue-jumper had caused quite a stir. She was much too lovely a sight to behold for anyone to feel annoyed at being held up. A foretaste of paradise, that's what she was. Most welcome, indeed.

Oblivious to the horde of heaven-hopeful rubberneckers eyeing her up from behind, Satan pursed her lips and waited. Her gaze was unflinching.

The saint hedged.

'However, if you feel strongly – and despite, I might add, a balance sheet that unequivocally destines him for your realm – if you nevertheless feel strongly, as you seem to insist, that this man is *not* in your purview, then I invite you to take the matter up with God himself.'

The man of God harrumphed. What realm, he contemptuously wondered, could possibly be in the purview of this woman? No offence to the devil, but she was, in his opinion – duly underscored by the unconscionable provocations with which she'd excruciated him – immeasurably more wicked.

'My dear Peter,' sighed Satan, softening suddenly. 'Must you be so punctilious? Stop being bound by your ridiculous, procedural rigmarole. Just take him back. You know very well he's a man of God.'

The Almighty pulled at his chin. There was no avoiding it. She was on her way up.

Could he bluff it out? *He was never on our payroll.*

No, he knew her too well; she wouldn't buy it.

Not on your payroll? Of course he was, she'd retort. *Every rule he brought to bear, every judgement he handed down, every damnation he dished out, he did in your name. Never once did you intervene to stop him. Your acquiescence makes him yours – irrefutably, indisputably, irrevocably.*

'Confound it! Am *I* to blame?' he roared, sanctimoniously indignant. Heaven's upper stratosphere reverberated with his rancour. Yet just as suddenly, with self-defeating honesty, he shamefacedly conceded the truth: 'Confound it: I AM.'

God, how he hated having to admit it. It was the damnedest thing about Truth: even he couldn't fake it. And his consort Satan knew it.

'Drat, drat, and triple drat. Why did I ever start this folly?'

More to the point, why was the road to perdition paved with good intentions? This had all started with Adam, Eve, and that accursed tree. Wishing only to shelter them from future sorrow, he had warned them off eating of its fruit. He'd only fudged a little. Satan, though, was scathing.

'*You?* God Almighty? You *lied*? How could you!'

'I only lied a little. For their own good.'

'Oh, that's rich! A fine example you set. And you think they're going to heed your dictum?'

'They'll heed it. They listen to me. They do what I say.'

'There's no reason why they should. And if they don't?'

'I'll give them hell, of course. Though I don't see what you mean. They have every reason to do as I say. After all, my goodwill is the sine qua non for the perks they get. They're not dim-witted. Why sabotage their own happiness?'

'*I* wouldn't put it past them. Especially now. Bravo!'

'Oh, ye of little faith,' tut-tutted God. 'They can eat all they like of the other trees. Just not the one I decreed off limits.'

'For a spurious reason! Death isn't the risk. It's dualism: dividing the world into right and wrong, good and evil, black and white. If they eat of that tree, they'll end up arguing opposites. They'll forfeit being whole. They'll find themselves outside of life, forever separated and looking in – whereas a state of blissful oneness with creation is their birthright. But only for so long as they forswear our divine fall from grace.'

'Precisely,' rejoined God. 'That's why I said they mustn't eat of that tree. If they do, *whoosh!* – Pandora's cat jumps out of the bag… I mean that figuratively, of course.'

'Oh for heaven's sake. Cats aren't the problem, my dear, neither Pandora's nor anyone else's. It's Judgement that's the problem. *Judgement creates good and evil.*'

'And I say it again: precisely! That's what I want to protect them from. After all, it is a sort of death, wouldn't you say, being cut off from life? That's why I said they'd die.'

Only what he'd said wasn't strictly true, and his having uttered an untruth, however slight, set an ungodly precedent. Goading him about his deceit – *Good luck playing King-of-the-moral-high-ground now!* – Satan had nonetheless acknowledged that if he were to openly admit he'd stretched the truth, his standing in all Creation would be jeopardized: *Once they suspect you of employing metaphors, they'll start interpreting everything you say.* She suggested he correct the misinformation in a surreptitious manner.

'And how might I do that?' enquired God, peeved that she knew better.

'By disguising yourself, of course. Find a costume to wear,

or change your form entirely. Hang out in the tree. Next time Eve or Adam comes round, be a sly little devil and clue them in. It doesn't matter from where the truth comes, so long as they get it. Lies are a blight on creation.'

'It was the only senseful thing she said, I must say; on *that* score, Saint Peter, God's Holy Spirit put Truth in her mouth. For *your* benefit, no doubt. Still, she's a she-devil to be sure, of the worst stripe. It's not to her you should be proposing an audience with the Almighty, but to *me* – a man of God!'

The passageway was inordinately long. The saint was annoyed with the power: every time his winged attendant went down to Hell, he came back in a sorry state. Once again, he'd begged off. The chore had fallen to him.

'Button it, will you?'

'How dare you! Hold my tongue? Never! But go on. Keep adding grist to the mill. You'll get your comeuppance when God hears how you've treated me.'

The man of God prattled on while the erstwhile fisherman, feeling nostalgic for his once simple life in Galilee, led the way to Purgatory. He'd locked the Pearly Gates and hung a sign: *Away on official business. Will return shortly.*

'Although frankly, S.P., I don't mind. A little trial and tribulation never hurts. Keeps one humble. Not that I'm lacking in humility. My followers have been praising me for years. They assure me I'm the most godly man the world has ever seen. I don't think it immodest to avow they're in no way exaggerating. After all, you have to consider the times. Take Jesus. His big exploit? Resisting temptation in a desert. How do you think he'd fare in today's profane world? Don't kid yourself! He'd be carried away by a simoom of sin faster than you could nail him to a cross to save his soul. Let's face it: only a man of God like myself, with moral fibres steeled in the spiritual furnace of God's own Law, can run the gauntlet of today's salacious seductions and emerge unscathed.

'Yet *my* record – which *you,* Saint Peter, seem to have suppressed, I dare say out of jealousy – my record testifies to my blamelessness. I have always tended God's precious flock as if it were my own. I have kept my sheep to the straight and narrow. I have punished those who transgress God's Inviolable Law and praised those who, in imitation of my shining example, apply themselves to separating good wheat from worthless chaff. Thanks to me and my loyal followers, God's flock is unerringly purged of abject sinners. Our effectiveness, I'm sure, has greatly simplified your work. No time wasted loading up the scales. Our judgement is sound. You can always count on our verdict as proof they're deserving of Hell. And good riddance!'

Saint Peter took a deep breath and steadied his nerves. It was a long trek to Purgatory.

'If only I'd left well enough alone,' God muttered to himself.

Oh, he'd played his part to the hilt. Donned the guise of a serpent. Jolly good fun. Scaly skin, muscle-bound coils, wise eyes. Having slinked up into the tree, he'd draped himself in its branches. Eve soon wandered by. He drew her attention with a sibilant come-on.

'Pssst. PssST! PSsssTT!'

That pulled her up short. Eve regarded her serpentine interlocutor with benevolent inquisitiveness.

'Are you *hissing* at me?'

'No. I was trying to whistle.'

'It's too sibilant,' she replied, frank to a fault. 'Try pursing your lips more.' She came closer. 'What do you want?'

God took his time. It was a question of rapport; he knew he'd have to first gain her confidence before she'd take him at his word in his present form. He asked numerous questions about her and Adam's life in the garden. How were they getting on? Did they mind the phases of the moon? Were they getting enough to eat? When to this Eve innocently replied, *We can eat the fruit of any tree in the garden, save this one, here in the middle. God told us we must not eat of this tree, or we will die,* the reptilian locum tenens casually seized his chance.

'Tut-tut. Really? He couldn't have meant that. I can assure you, the truth is less ominous. No one dies from eating this fruit.'

'You're just a snake,' said Eve dismissively. 'What would you know? You don't even eat fruit. God told us we'd die. Snakes can't speak for God.'

Unaccustomed to being humbled, he drew himself up.

'Don't be so quick to dismiss what I say. I speak the Truth.'

'I doubt it. You've got a forked-tongue.'

How dare she, thought God, nettled by her shrewd wit. *I'll show her. I'll wow her with the whole shebang.*

'My forked-tongue in no way disqualifies me from speaking the Truth,' he countered. 'God had his reasons, no doubt, for obfuscating the matter, but the truth is this: the day you eat of this tree's fruit, not only will you not die, but your eyes will be opened. You will see as you never saw before. In fact, you will be like God – you will be in the Know, with Knowledge of Good and Evil. You'll be able to judge for yourselves and tell them apart.'

How do you like them apples, Eve? He wasn't lying now. It was true, all true! Every word. *Ha! Let her weigh the pros and cons of that,* he triumphantly hissed to himself. Confident that he'd set the record straight and righted his wrong, God wove his way down the trunk and slithered off into the garden, holding his head high. They now had full disclosure – nothing hidden, nothing omitted. As such, Adam and Eve were at perfect liberty to make an informed choice. His consort Satan was unpersuaded, but God had faith: once their two beloved spitting images had turned things over in their minds, he was sure they'd choose the elations of guileless, happy wholeness over the pernicious torments of relentless discernment.

Satan was taking in the room, her roaming eye made avid by absence. Little had changed. The wall where her portrait had once hung opposite God's own was as bare as the day she'd left. She felt a giddy twinge of hope.

'Miss me?'

God noted her impish smile. Did he miss her? Of course. Terribly. But admit as much? He kept his own counsel.

Their estrangement had been, quite simply, a collateral upshot of all that had followed his tiny, well-intentioned lie. Satan, with soft-hearted sympathy for Eve and Adam's freely exercised choice, had wisely said, *Let's wait and see.* God, pricked in his pride, had riposted, *Wait'll they see!* Curiosity was no warrant, temptation no excuse. All of creation could see they'd disregarded his injunction. Insubordination called for consequences. It had to be nipped in the bud, lest – *monkey see, monkey do* – the monkeys followed suit. Overruling his consort's bent for leniency, he passed sentence with a vengeance. He kicked them out of Eden.

But once kicked, there was no stopping mankind. Hellbent on multiplying their footprint on Earth in record time, they were soon sowing their good-natured mischief to the four winds with abandon. They stopped obeying him altogether. God lost his temper again and unleashed a tabula rasa flood to stem the tide of their waywardness. Conscience-stricken following that unholy cataclysm, he'd tried to coax the various remnants to heel with a string of everlasting covenants: time and again, he offered them an olive branch; time and again, the scions of Eve and Adam's loins beat their breasts in repentence; time and again, they unfailingly went off to do once again exactly as they pleased. Why, they became adept at scheming newfangled ways to get his divine goat. It drove him to distraction.

'What makes you think your man belongs with me?' asked Satan, settling herself down in her old armchair and making herself at home. God's portrait, still hanging on the wall behind his own chair, gazed at her. That face shone with divine felicity; the face before her was careworn and haggard.

'His record speaks for that. It's as clear as day.'

'Poppycock. His record makes clear that everything he did, he did in your name,' she retorted, playing with one of her long, auburn curls. 'He's a pure product, my dear, of your ever-failing efforts to re-bag Pandora's cat. You take him.'

'I won't. He belongs in Hell.'

'Well I'm not going to take him. Put him in your Purgatory playpen with the others.'

God surmised she knew he was already there. He frowned.

'Why can't you see reason?'

'Why can't you admit you were wrong?'

God had sent his heavenly gatekeeper to the other-worldly boondocks with clear instructions. *Keep an eye on him. Don't let him out of your sight. I'll send word as soon as she relents.*

So it was that Saint Peter was now twiddling his thumbs and looking down over a vast congregation of souls, all men of God. He shivered. These furthest recesses of Purgatory were frigid with cold-heartedness.

It was easy to see that not one holier-than-thou had the slightest clue as to why he'd been sidelined in limbo. Talking shop, arguing exegetical nuances, reminiscing about sinners they'd caught red-handed and verdicts they'd rendered, they milled about in formularised paths that always led them to but one conclusion: God in Heaven was asleep at the helm.

There were cliques of all cloths. There were followers of Bahá'u'lláh; of Confucius; of Gurū Nānak; of Joseph Smith; of Lao-tzu; of Moses; of Muhammad; of Christ; of Rumi; of Siddhārtha Gautama; of Zoroaster. You'd have thought these denizens of divergent orthodoxies would be at ideological daggers drawn, yet it was nothing of the sort; indeed, quite to the contrary, once they'd compared notes they found to their surprise they were as akin as peas in a pod: they knew they were right. Recognizing themselves as all being cut from the very same cloth, they unreservedly united in common cause; and when their vaunted acme of integrity, that most supremely pious man of God, was roughly show in by their nemesis – that lunatic gate-saint – they decried the injustice with one voice.

His predeceased devotees ran to succour him.

'Master! Master! What is this? How is it possible? You? Here? Of all of us, you, surely, deserve to be in Heaven!'

They helped the man of God to his feet.

'O, my fellow faithful,' he sighed, 'how good it is to see you again. There is no greater solace than injustice shared.'

They pressed him for news. He related to them his tale of being ignominiously bounced from the Pearly Gates; of being trussed up like a turkey by a cross-dressing lackey and bundled into a lift; of being subjected to abominable excruciations at the claws of a she-devil who cachinnated unceasingly at his expense. His listeners were aghast. How to make sense of this topsy-turvy turning of the tables? How to account for a man of God – a man such as *he*, the very epitome of rectitude – being packed off not just to the furthest reaches of Purgatory as they had been, but to the deepest unknown bowels of the Earth, perhaps to the gateway of Hell itself? Something was surely amiss. They begged him to elucidate. He did not disappoint.

'My friends, as I was being so gratuitously escorted to this abominable dell of darkness brightened only by your shining countenances, it occurred to me that something is not right in the Holy Realms. It cannot have escaped your attention. That *you* are here is damning evidence there has been an unpardonable miscarriage of God's Will.'

'Hear, hear!' cried the congregation as one.

'But that *I* should be sent here,' he continued, sharpening his tongue, 'is incontrovertible proof, if I may be so bold – and I will – *that Almighty God has lost His Marbles.*'

The burst of mirth that greeted this witty barb belied the sincerity with which the gathered men of God all began nodding in unqualified agreement.

Striking while the iron was hot, the man of God launched an impromptu bid for a schismatic coup de ciel.

'Patriarchs! Rabbis! Imams! Lend me your ears! I am sure you agree – there is but one Law: God's Law. For whom did the Lord God make Heaven? For those He loves! And whom does God love? Those who, upholding His Holy Strictures, ordain them for all, for their own good. And Hell? For whom did He Most Mighty make Hell? Yes! For those He hates! And whom does God hate? Those who baulk at His Holy Precepts and refuse to toe His Line. It is God's LAW: the Good go Up, the Evil go Down!

'What can it therefore mean if – rather than lauded for our peerless merits and rushed to our heavenly rewards – we find ourselves today sequestered in the dank confines of this dismal limbo?'

He paused while an aggrieved murmur made the rounds.

'There is no beating around the bush. It can mean but one thing,' he concluded, pointing an accusatory finger in Saint Peter's direction: *'He and his ilk have deposed God!'*

A roar of indignation went up, rebounding off the vault. Had the man of God not called them to restraint, the congregation as a whole would have clawed their way to the balcony on the spot and torn Saint Peter to shreds.

'No, my children! No! Spare him for now. Do not bother. I will see to it that every sinful agent of rebellion against God gets his just desserts – especially our mutinous Mr Key!'

A joyful feeling of brotherhood gladdened the gathering. The men of God pressed closer to their saviour.

'Yes! Put your faith in me! I will find a way to right what is wrong. There can be no doubt: the heavenly host has led the Almighty astray with lies and deceit. Why, it may even be that God Himself has been corrupted…'

A breathless gasp.

'But wait! Even if these miscreants have rendered the One True God Himself impure, do not fear! Are we not ourselves a bastion of all that is Holy and Righteous? If God has been robbed of His purity of Soul, let no one fear: We will take His Place. We will step in to save His Creation from ruin. As it has been on Earth during our tenure, so it will be in Heaven – and there will be rejoicing, or we will know the reason why!'

A deafening cheer erupted. Shouts of *Yes! Yes! You will save us all! You must sit on God's throne! You must take His Place!* rang out.

'You are too kind, my friends, too kind! If it comes to that, I will submit to your will. But for the time being, should we not in all modesty hope that God will find His Marbles? Surely, when God hears the Truth from our lips, he will not rest until He Himself has seen that we are all of us seated in our rightful place, in thrones by His Side. Nor will He who loves us as He loves Himself fail to punish those who have thwarted His Will and barred our entry to Heaven. He who is like a Father to us – nay, who *is* our Father – will not…'

The man of God was on a roll, inspired by the rapt adulation with which his fellow men of the cloth were receiving his every word. Saint Peter saw he'd have no better opportunity to slip away unseen. Easing himself into the shadows, he felt his way to the door. Once safely inside the secret passage, he bolted the portal securely shut, turned on his heel, and threw himself into a race against time up the passageway.

❧

Why on Earth had he laid down laws? Why hadn't he had the good sense to simply accept that Eve and Adam, no less than he and Satan, were perfectly free to do as they pleased? Why should it matter? But no. All to assuage his wounded pride, he'd singled out a small tribe on which to pin his high hopes for some semblance of deference and tractability, and in so doing unwittingly hurled the whole of creation down an ever steepening, slippery slope with a millstone round its neck – a millstone made heavier by each passing generation, for they could not refrain from multiplying his laws in diabolical ways. He'd thought ten from the get-go would amply cover their needs. They had a finger for each to remember them by. As he'd joked at the time, *If they lose a finger, I'll let them off the hook for the law it represents – but only if they know for which law it stood.* Only he hadn't foreseen that some navel-gazing priest would look further than his willy and decide that ten more could be added, one for each toe on the heels of the first. Tacked on in clear violation of God's command to not add one iota to what he'd set down in stone, that first wave of exponential doubling never stopped.

Satan divined his thoughts.

'You realise that the present state of affairs all stems from those tablets you gave them?'

Her companion said nothing.

'We'd still be together as we were in the beginning, if you hadn't given their offspring those laws to play with.'

'They weren't supposed to play with them. They were supposed to obey them.'

'Oh. Like Eve and Adam? Good precedent.'

It was a sore point for God. He glowered.

'All I know,' she went on, 'is that they got so enamoured with laws and statutes and decrees and precedents and canons and dictums and edicts and rulings, to say nothing of capital punishments and penances and penalties inflicted on those they judged to have transgressed those laws, that you and I were driven apart. They imprisioned you up here in Heaven, tasking you with welcoming those who toed their lines, and sent me down to Hell, where I've been comforting the myriad others who fell foul of their clutches ever since.'

'I send all the ones who think they deserve Heaven to Purgatory. It's overflowing with pastoral do-gooders.'

'And who do you have in Heaven? Those to whom your laws don't apply: the children. But no one else. And why? Because no one truly worth their salt has ever been able to hold to your ten commandments. Jesus and I were talking about it just the other day. He's a lovely soul, by the way. He's made himself very much at home. We all love him dearly. Augustine too, I might add, now that he's realised how often and badly he erred; today he's an enthusiastic champion of love without regard nor compunction for its many forms and guises. Such a shame for you, that they and so many others couldn't pass muster in your book.'

Didn't he know it. Once he'd chiseled out his law, God had felt honour-bound to uphold it. That too was pride. All he'd done was compound his original mistake ad infinitum.

'Dearest,' said Satan, leaning forward and taking her consort's hand in hers. 'Listen to me. We can change this. Long ago, we imagined ourselves all-knowing. We were naive. We joined, as one, but we did not fathom union. We created, as gods, but we did not comprehend creation. We loved, as lovebirds, but we did not understand love.

'This I have learned since: there is only union, creation, and love. These three are One – and in their mysterious midst, in their dance without end, all Life resides.'

He knew she was right. In the beginning, they'd been in perfect harmony – evolving, expanding, the magic they wrought boundless, unstoppable. But all that had changed. They'd lost it all. How had they strayed so far?

As if reading his thoughts, she went on.

'Our original sin, my dear, was to eat of the tree of knowledge. No sooner did that cursed fruit open our eyes than – to our inconsolable horror, you might recall – everything we looked upon became in our sight either black or white, good or evil, right or wrong. Embracing judgement, we abandoned love. Abandoning love, we fell from grace.'

He remembered the suddenness of that fall all too well.

'Sadly, there's no going back,' he sighed. 'At this point, I'm sure I could never cease to judge. Pandora's cat, and all that.'

He gave her a glum wink.

'And that's where you're wrong,' chirped Satan, giving his hand a squeeze. 'You should pay more attention to what Eve and Adam's offspring have to say now and then. Some are quite wise indeed. Too often their words are overtaken and cruelly twisted by well-intentioned but unenlightened disciples with a visceral need to add their own two cents; even worse are the latecomers who never knew them in the first place and yet feel entitled to speak reams of rubbish in their name. But if you stick to the original message and tune out all the commentary and exegesis propounded in its wake, then I can assure you of this: they know how to put Pandora's silly cat back in the sack.'

❧

They were interrupted by Saint Peter's arrival. All out of breath, he barged in unannounced.

'Confound it, Peter! What brings you here? I said I'd send word. We haven't yet finished with the negotiations.'

'My poor Peter,' said Satan, rising to her feet and smiling sweetly. 'For heaven's sake, you look as though you've had a fright. Here, take my seat. I'll get you some holy water.'

Satan went off to fetch a glass as Saint Peter gratefully settled himself into her chair's soft upholstery.

'Well? I'm waiting. Why are you here?'

'Let me catch my breath,' panted Peter, all out of wind.

God was supremely annoyed but said nothing as the saint filled his lungs with heaven's ether. The glass of holy water duly revived his spirits, and Satan seated herself on the arm of her chair. She and God were all ears as Saint Peter related the events he had witnessed in the nether regions of Purgatory. The tale of what was brewing in limbo went from bad to worse. By the end, God was sitting on the edge of his seat, dismayed and aghast.

'At that point,' said Peter, concluding his report, 'I grabbed my chance to slip away. I felt it was imperative that you hear what's afoot. For now, we're safe; the portal is barred; no one will escape. But the next time a man of God comes pounding on the Pearly Gates, what then? We'll have to haul him down to Purgatory and open the door to boot him inside where he belongs with the others… and believe you me, there'll be no stopping the lot of them from swarming.'

The prospect was harrowing. God slumped back into his chair.

'This is unholy,' he said darkly. 'I won't have it. How dare they. They're provoking me. I'm going to smite them once and for all.'

'You'll do nothing of the sort,' scolded Satan. 'It's beneath you. You've never smitten anyone. This is no time to start.'

'I don't see why not,' huffed God. 'Besides, they started it. They've been smiting their enemies for centuries. It's high time they got a taste of what they so freely dish out.'

'Nonsense. Besides, it won't cure them. You'd probably make a hash of it, too. Who's going to clean up after you?'

Peter shifted uneasily in the chair. The power was still indisposed.

Standing up to stretch her legs, Satan began wandering in random circles of thought. She knew she would find what she was looking for when it found her first.

Saint Peter felt sorry for them both. Although he wasn't privy to all the metaphysical ins and outs of God and Satan's binary complementarity, he'd gleaned enough to gather that their power as gods had been severely curtailed following their separation. Mankind had occupied the breach ever since, calling the shots in supposed league with one or the other when in fact they were beholden to no one's will but their own. Heaven and hell had been created at the instigation of so-called holy men for the sole purpose of keeping God and Satan separated ever since.

'To think he imagined I'd welcome him with open arms,' grumbled God. 'What? Is he clueless? Does he really think he's a model of virtue? The sanctimonious nerve! And with a gala reception, no less. Trumpets a-blaring and finger food galore! I should be so gullible.'

'What's that you say?' piped up Satan, turning on her heel.

'I said, *I should be so gullible.* But I mean it the other way, of course: I'm *not* that gullible.'

'No, I mean about finger food and trumpets. What's this about a gala reception?'

His acolytes were on tenterhooks.

'When?'

'Soon. Very soon.'

'Will we be included?'

'I'll see what I can do.'

It was an invitation-only, RSVP affair. The man of God had responded, *Long overdue, but I'll forgive the slight. Please inform the caterers that, even as a child, I was allergic to shellfish. Let them take note, if they value their position.*

'What about the key-twirling saint?' said one, disgruntled that Peter had so blithely dismissed his numerous appeals as inadmissible. 'Will he still be in charge?'

'Don't you worry, my friend,' said the man of God with smug certainty. 'The demotion of Saint Fishbreath will be the object of my first Angelica Coelestis Bulla.'

His acolytes were all smiles. The tables were turning!

With fawning attentions, they helped the man of God don the ceremonial regalia that had been sent down along with the embossed invitation. They were gladdened to see no expense had been spared. The cloth, silky to the touch, was of the finest weave, the robes seamless and spotlessly white. It was about time their mentor and master be shown proper consideration. To all evidence, God had found His Marbles. The game was on!

Just then, Saint Peter appeared at the balcony. Glaring up at him, the malcontent votaries growled menacingly. The saint ignored them. With solemn and grave demeanour, he placidly unrolled a parchment scroll and began to read.

'Hear ye! Hear ye! Verily, verily! God has spoken! Let all who love Truth come near! The very portals of Heaven are henceforth thrown open to receive God's own, one Reginald Faysal Hatim Dempster. Let he who in life was beloved by his toady minions as an unimpeachable vessel of virtue – yet rebuked by his victims as an obstinately bigoted cesspool of priggish piety and noxious dogma – come forth from the tenebrous depths of Purgatory, where the reader of this holy promulgation – namely, myself, Saint Peter, sinner that I am – so heinously consigned him. Let God's Man on Earth harken to God's Call from Heaven. *Come forth,* sayeth He, *and claim thy rightful place, for thyself and thy followers.*'

Yes! Their time had come, too! With an indecorous whoop of triumph, the congregation below broke into a free-for-all frenzy of dancing joy that rattled the rafters, accompanied by thunderous hurrahs of victory.

Deftly giving turn to a hand-cranked wheel, Saint Peter proceeded to lower an extensible stairway from the balcony. When it touched the floor of Purgatory, he carefully set the safety catch and pointed to God's chosen one.

Entranced by the import of the moment, those blocking the way to their guiding light's imminent ascension all stepped aside to clear a path, bowing their heads reverentially as he went forth, one measured step at a time, his face aglow with self-admiration, his heart more than happy to squeeze the occasion for all it was worth. Reaching the stairs, he took hold of the flimsy guardrail and mounted the first step. His fellows were fast on his heels, eager to follow in his footsteps.

Saint Peter held up his hand.

'You're the only invitee for this occasion. It said so on the invitation.'

Emboldened by the turn of events, the man of God stood firm and played to the gallery.

'I protest! I will not leave one single lamb behind,' he declared. With a sweeping gesture he added, 'If *I* go, *they* go!'

Saint Peter threw the safety catch. In two shakes, the stairway returned to the balcony, carrying the man of God with it and leaving the herd in the dust.

'Listen up,' advised Saint Peter under his breath, conveying with a hard look he meant every word. 'Play ball, or I'll push you over the railing. No VIP carpet. No redemption.'

The man of God made a quick calculation.

'What about my flock?'

'Their fate is tied to yours.'

'You mean – ?'

'Precisely.'

'And I'll be able to – ?'

'Indubitably.'

'With free rein? According to my own lights?'

'Such is God's plan.'

'Ha! What did I tell you? I know the Mind of the Creator better than anyone. I knew I'd get Heaven's highest honour. When will I be made sovereign potentate of the flock?'

'One thing at a time. Formalities first. You'd do well to reassure them. You'll reunite with them soon.'

The man of God turned and raised his hands in a call for silence. His bleating followers grudgingly reined in their unbridled indignation. The brouhaha died down. The congregation was all ears.

'My fellow luminaries and beacons of virtue! As we each and every one of us know, we alone are God's Chosen Ones,' intoned the man of God, addressing them as equals from his privileged perch on the balcony. 'But as He has done before – I'm thinking here of Moses, of Paul, of Muhammad the Holy Prophet – God in His Infinite Wisdom has singled me out for a most special rôle in His Own Divine Plan. You yourselves heard the holy promulgation. God has called me today to claim my rightful place; but not *my* place only; *thy* place as well! Our fiend here, Peter, has just confirmed that I am to be accorded full powers to reverse the villainous verdicts with which he and his clique tarred you. Your liberation from Purgatory is assured, your trials and tribulations will soon end. I therefore ask you to be patient. For now, be of good cheer. Keep faith a while longer. I will ascend to Heaven and undergo their induction rigmarole. As soon as God has duly accredited my position as Keeper of the Flock, as I am assured He intends to do, I will exercise my full authority in Heaven as I have always done on Earth. My Bulls will put order in God's House; My Judgements will ensure that Heaven is peopled only by souls who meet our highest standards; and My Wrath will damn all those who dare oppose us!'

Cheers erupted. A tidal wave of euphoria swept over the crowd.

'It's time,' said Saint Peter, tapping him on the shoulder.

'I'll be with you in a moment,' whispered the man of God,

basking in his confrères' ad libitum veneration.

With the forbearance of a fisherman, Saint Peter doled out a wee measure of slack. *Go ahead*, he thought to himself – *run with it. After all, this is my last mission. I can wait.*

Packed to overflowing, Heaven's celestial amphitheatre was thronged with angels of all stripes and wing configurations sitting wingtip to elbow with white-robed attendees from all walks of former lives. The elbowees were unhappy about the robes they had to wear, but the event had been billed as formal attire only: *Nudity*, the invite had read, *is ruled unsuited for this occasion.*

Among the robe-clad crowd, there was no end to the sight of faces hitherto unseen in the heavenly realms. Being familiar with each other, of course, they were soon feeling right at home in their new surroundings. Not a few of the wing-tipped bevy were familiar faces as well; it had been a blanket amnesty all around. Indeed, they'd cleared out for good from their old abode and left it immaculate in their wake for the incoming tenants.

The event had been organized in accordance with God's wishes, with preparations left to Saint Peter's stewardship: '*Go to town, Mr P – as gaudy as you like. Sky's the limit.*'

The saint had given free rein to his imagination. Taking his cue from the Temple rites he'd seen in Jerusalem all those millennia ago, he'd combined well-ordered grandeur with the wondrous tales he'd heard of Roman pomp and drawn up a blueprint for the event that had tickled Satan pink.

'Why, you've outdone yourself, Peter,' she enthused. 'No more key-rattling for you. *Emcee of Eternity*, that'll be your gig from now on.'

Peter surveyed the scene. She was right. He had outdone himself. Greater resplendence than this was inconceivable.

It was time to start the show.

'Holy! holy! holy!' he intoned, his voice reverberating in tempo with the twinkling stars overhead as he cued God for his almighty grand entrance. 'Let us make our reverence to the One, the Only, G-O-D,' boomed Peter – 'the Great G-O-D, under whose blessed aegis we are gathered here to-day. Let's hear it for the Lord!'

A deafening peal of hallelujahs greeted His Divineship as God stepped from the shadows into the limelight. With good-humoured devotion, the prankish members of the host immediately started chanting *G-O-D-G-O-D-G-O-D-G-O-D-G-O-D-O-G-D-O-G-D-O-* and soon had the entire amphitheatre in stitches with their favourite pun. The newcomers were delighted to discover that Dío G himself got a kick out of the ribbing.

'Thank you! Thank you! You're too kind,' laughed God, once the foot stomping and mirth had subsided. 'I love you. You're wooferful. Please, be seated. Thank you.'

The crowd settled down and hushed itself in gleeful expectation. God beamed with genuine rapture. This was fun. Surveying the seemingly endless sea of hopeful faces, he was touched. The long-awaited Judgement Day had finally come.

He began in earnest.

'My angelic compeers and immortal counterparts! As befits this stupendous mise en scène, so lovingly concocted by our former Gate Bouncer and Keeper of the Holy Keys, we are gathered here today for a unique occasion. Never before have we had reason to host a ceremony like this. Today, we will confer on the greatest ever self-appointed Man of God – a Man of God, I might add, such as we hope to never see again – an honour to match his self-aggrandizing humility and his self-lauded virtue. We will vouchsafe him a rank that most deservedly is his, a status he has earned in spades and a moniker that suits him to a T.

'You here present, in your heart of hearts, know that not one of you ever came close to matching his unenviable record of hard-line exaction. Be it precept or tenet, commandment or rule, our Man of God cut no slack: to flout the smallest of punctilios was to plummet from his grace, to contravene but one jot of Law was to incur his unforgiving wrath. He brooked no deviation, bore no difference of opinion. His view, Truth! His reckoning, Right! His teaching, Gospel!'

A ripple of merriment greeted these words. The noxious notions were so jarringly counterfeit that one could only snicker at the incongruity.

'Do you know what he did, our most earnest Man of God? Brandishing his Trinity of Twaddle, he made it his business to goad and browbeat humanity as a whole into submission to Me. Yes, to *me!* And on *my* behalf, no less! Oh, you can all imagine how grateful I am to him for *that*,' said God with wry sincerity, sparking off more fits of giggles and not a few guffaws.

'Yes, yes, on *my* behalf,' continued God, pantomiming a nod of amazement. 'On *my* behalf, *and in My Name*. Heaven help me. No wonder, then, that it means so much to me – yes, to Me, God Himself – to reward him for his alacritous zeal.

'Now, I know that some of you here present – need I cite names? I'm thinking of certain freewheeling messiahs, certain lotus-flower-powered ascetics, certain ruminant poets! – eventually shed the hand-me-down rules on which you'd been weaned. Sometimes sooner, sometimes later, you discovered for yourselves that law is antithetical to love. Indeed, once free of Law, you divined that *Love* – unfettered, uncharted and unassumingly unashamed – is the only path to Paradise.

'I do solemnly admit and confess: to have saddled you with Law is my Original Sin. It is I, God, who cut you off from Paradise… and in so doing, I cut my own Self off from my one True Love, my Beloved Consort. I have pined away for Her ever since in my lonely, ivory tower; while She – expelled from Heaven by spurious holy men and exiled to a hypogeal abode – took you in, cared for you, and sustained you. From Her you have learned Love. It is She who made you worthy to be here today. And not you only, but me as well… for which I am most humbly grateful.'

Turning to where Satan was seated, God gave her a rueful smile. In reply, her eyes twinkled with love and the assurance that all was forgiven. So encouraged, and in decidedly happy anticipation of delights to come, God pursued his oration.

'For Us, then, One and All, together at last, the Kingdom of that heavenly Paradise called Love. Let us partake therein fully.

'But what of our Man of God? I said I would reward him for his zeal. And reward he shall have,' proclaimed God. 'No less than a kingdom all his own. And more than just a kingdom. He shall have his own flock. Yes! A flock all his own…'

God was dubious.

'You don't think I laid it on too thick?'

'You were perfect. Everyone loved it.'

'I wasn't too long-winded?'

'Of course you were. But it fitted the occasion. After all, it was a one-off. We'll never have need for it again, so long as we remember our lesson.'

God and Satan were lying together in perfect, post-coital bliss. Oh, it had been so long! Both the bliss, and the waiting they'd endured leading up to it. How many aeons, come and gone? How many seasons, frittered away? They had both feared their separation would last forever. Yet their deepest desires never flagged, their wildest hopes never dimmed. To think they were here – at last! – together again. It was a miracle. Love had triumphed over Death. Love had brought them back to Life. Love had returned them to each other.

'We'll remember, so long as we keep faith. In love.'

'Yes. In Love. Not Law.'

Cooling his heels in the amphitheatre's undercrofts and cupping his ear in hopes of catching a snatch of God's speech, the man of God had flushed with excitement as he awaited his empyreal elevation. *Truly*, he thought, *God works in mysterious ways.* He understood it all now: his bitter if thankfully brief taste of Purgatory had been but a spiritual palate-cleanser, a depurative hors-d'œuvre served up to render his ascension to Heaven all the more sweet. Wholly unnecessary, of course; purgation was fare better suited to flagellatory friars, not faultless apotheoses such as he; there where imperfect postulants deserved just deserts, apogees of saintliness like himself should be served heaping helpings of ambrosia. But why quibble with God's bill of fare? What mattered now was his ascension. Besides, the affronts he'd suffered at the hands of God's maître key had endeared him to his followers all the more. Incensed by the injustices to which their unassailable lodestar had been subjected, they were primed and fired to follow him anywhere.

Saint Peter and the power arrived to escort him to the amphitheatre.

'All set?' asked the saint. 'Ready to reap your reward? There's a big crowd up there in the bleachers, all on tenterhooks. They've been waiting a hellishly long time for this moment. They can hardly wait to see your numberless virtues requited.'

'Yes, well, their waiting is at an end. As I've always said, justice will out – and I've never been wrong. But since you ask, I wouldn't be honest if I said were feeling a wee bit nervous,' said the man of God with supreme confidence and a complacent smile – 'so I won't.'

They helped him to adjust his robes, ensuring they fell in graceful folds. Appearances were important.

'No last minute regrets? No pangs of remorse? Qualms of conscience?'

'Ha! Surely not. But what about you? Doesn't it make *you* dizzy, to realize that I – a born saint who never once aspired to be more nor less than a humble man of God, content with repressing sin per the dictates of my perfect perspicacity – should have so spectacularly surpassed all others, including your hapless friend, that Galilean gadabout? I mean, given my tireless, lifelong crusade in defence of God's Law, it's no wonder I've always cut a godlier figure than my contemporaries. But to have even outshone the likes of Jesus? Now, that's a feat! You have to admit, it's a pretty jewel that's going to top *my* crown.'

The power looked away and rolled his eyes, but Peter kept a straight face. Ignoring the fact that celestial crowns were a purely fallacious construct, the saint humoured him all the same.

'Yes, you'll certainly have a pretty crown jewel. We're all quite envious.'

'As well you should be,' crowed the man of God magnanimously. '*You*, He put in charge of a latchkey; *Me*, a flock of fellow champions of His Most Holy Law. By any measure, it's clear that God loves me more than you.'

The opening bars of a triumphal ethereal march reached their ears. The time had come. The long-suffering saint took the lead as they headed up a dimly lit passageway that led to the vomitorium.

They came to the threshold.

'Here part our ways,' said the saint.

The man of God paused to pinch himself. Was all this for real? Why, yes! And so truly so! Just look where he stood: the Gateway to Glory! It had taken a lifetime to secure, but the pay-off was worth it. To him – at last! – his Supreme Consecration. To him – at last! – his Rightful Place. To him – verily and at last! – the Proof that He Stood on a Par with God.

He sighed with beatific sanctitude.

Saint Peter proffered a complaisant smile and a deferential bow.

'After you,' he said. 'May Hell enjoy the consequences.'

With a cheery nod of confident assent, the man of God, his step assured, went boldly forth.

The magnificent fig

Once upon a time, far from a town where the land's king and queen lived in a castle surrounded by a moat, there was a magnificent fig ripening on the branch of a solitary tree.

The fig was a beauty. The tree knew that in all her long life, she had never once produced a fruit as fine as this one. All her other figs were ripening in turn; some had ripened sooner, others would ripen later. And the birds were coming daily and singing her praises – for she was an isolated tree, and they were grateful for her bounty in that remote and seldom visited area.

But this particular fig was a treasure. It was ripening to perfection. No ant had crossed the stem to investigate its riches. No fruit fly had dared alight on the unblemished surface to feast and lay eggs in its fertile flesh. No bird had detected its presence, for the fruit was well hidden from sight by a dense spray of leaves. The fig's ripeness would soon reach its zenith – sheathed by the flawless skin, the glistening pulp would be lusciously sweet, the tiny seeds poised to play a delicate counterpoint to its inner leitmotif. The fig would be perfection incarnate, and the tree knew it.

'To think,' she lamented, 'that my greatest achievement will go unnoticed beyond my own little patch of world, where only birds sing my praises. What can birds know about perfection and beauty and exquisite finesse in a fig? When they come to feast, all they do is gorge themselves and splatter my leaves with droppings. Is there any tree more unhappy than I?'

When the harvest moon appeared in the east that evening, the tree was very sad.

Come the next morning, though, she heard footsteps that belonged to no animal who roamed regularly in those parts. To the tree's great surprise, a woman carrying a large wicker basket was tramping through the tall grass, making a beeline for her fig-laden branches.

Pausing briefly to catch her breath and to admire the tree's ample grandeur, the woman heartily congratulated herself for having dared to trek so far in search of figs. She soon hastened forward and began reaching for the ripe fruit. She ate as she worked, and after tasting a few, the woman knew she had found an uncommonly good tree.

'No two trees are alike, but never in my life have I tasted figs as toothsome as these. Such flavour! They're far and away superior to any of the figs closer to town. I'm sure to sell them all at market tomorrow, and for a good price, too. Oh! hello – '

She had pushed back the dense spray of protective leaves and discovered the magnificent fig.

'Gracious me – aren't you a peach!'

The woman marvelled at the fig.

'You're like no fig I've ever seen. Who's to say the king's men won't pay a handsome price for you. Yes, indeed…'

Mindful not to harm the fig's tender skin, she worked the stem free from the branch and came out from under the shade to admire her find more fully in the light.

'Good Lord, what a fig. I'd eat you myself if I weren't so poor, just to know what perfection tastes like. But the king's gold coin will make me a richer woman than I am today. And God knows I'm a poor woman.'

She wrapped the precious jewel in her kerchief and placed it on a soft bed of leaves beside her basket. Then she continued gathering figs from the branches of the majestic old tree, who couldn't have been more pleased.

'Imagine,' she rustled, 'the king himself might taste my fruit! And the queen might suggest they grant me their protection and blessing. Why, they'll probably fête me and cover me with honours. They'll name me *Royal Fig Tree of the Kingdom…*'

On she palavered, her leaves chattering chimeras while the woman picked all the figs that were ripe and within reach.

After an hour of toil, the woman had filled her basket with fruit. Placing her kerchief with the prize fig on top of all the rest, and carefully balancing the basket laden with its priceless treasure on her crown, she set off on her long walk back to the town and her home.

The following day, the woman arrived early at market to claim a good spot. The other vendors of figs and fruit eyed her lone basket, disdaining the poor woman with so little to offer; and wasn't she acting above herself, they thought, when they overheard the price she gave to a traveller who, no doubt out of pity, had stopped to inquire about her figs.

'That's surely a high price for figs,' he answered.

'Not for these, my lord,' she said, halving one of the choice figs with her knife. 'One taste and you'll know why, if you'll be so kind.'

When the vendors saw the look that came over the man's face as the fig melted in his mouth, they could scarcely believe their eyes. And when he paid on the spot without haggling the price – and then, not deigning even a cursory glance, walked past all their stands – they were sorely vexed. What figs were these that the woman had found?

Soon the king's chamberlain arrived with purse in hand, attended by a bevy of basket-bearing commis chefs to carry the day's provisions. The king and queen were returning that day from a tour of their kingdom and they were sure to be looking forward not only to regaining their castle, but to an evening meal prepared with the finest attentions and forethought for their pleasure. The chamberlain was on a mission to delight his royal lords.

As the coterie approached, the woman picked up her kerchief. Cradling it in her palm, she made a deliberate show of carefully pulling back the corners to reveal the magnificent fig.

'This is a fig fit for the king,' she declared, just as the chamberlain came level with where she sat.

The vendors interrupted their transactions to stare at the

fig. Their jaws dropped and they blinked. Seeing his usual vendors awestruck and speechless, the chamberlain stopped and followed their gaze. His eyes widened when he saw the fig.

'Fit for the king,' repeated the woman.

The chamberlain managed a nod but said not a word.

'I see you agree, my lord. But you want to be sure. Here, taste a sibling fig from the same tree.'

She held out the other half of the fig she had cut for the man who'd passed by before. The chamberlain's mouth watered as his fingers took the fruit; he brought the morsel to his lips; its fragrance filled his nostrils; and when his tongue discovered its succulent texture, its incomparable flavour, the memory of all other figs receded from his mind. Nothing could compare with what he was tasting, this symphony of honeyed goodness. The fig lying in the woman's kerchief would be that and so much more.

'It is my duty to procure this fig for His Majesty,' he said at last. 'How shall we agree on a price?'

The woman took hold of the corners of her kerchief, each in turn, and protectively covered the fig once more.

'My lord, both you and I know this fig is priceless. Perfection is a treasure that puts even gold to shame. I want only that our king should have the pleasure of this delicacy.'

She looked the chamberlain in the eye and he could only agree. He opened his purse and withdrew a heavy gold coin.

'May God keep you well.'

With a snap of his fingers to commandeer an empty basket, he himself took charge of the precious fig's conveyance.

Learning that the meal to be served that evening would be crowned with the finale of the fig, the chef concocted a menu worthy of a triumph. All afternoon, he harried his sous-chefs to perform culinary feats with the provisions that had been brought back from market. Fish were poached in court bouillon, lamb was roasted with fine herbs and drippings, tasty side dishes were prepared and garnished with pistachios and pine nuts. Meanwhile, under the chamberlain's watchful eye, the magnificent fig was placed on a porcelain platter and covered with a crystal dome, to be set on a well-guarded sideboard for safekeeping. The fruit blazed with beauty. All who passed paid reverence, knowing they would never again see a fig as lovely as the one destined for the king.

That evening, the entire culinary staff – the chef, the sous-chefs, the waiters and attendants – saw to their respective duties with devotion and alacrity. Seated each in their respective place at opposite ends of the banquet table, the king and queen regaled themselves as the kitchen sent forth an unprecedented procession of delectable dishes, each one striking a flawless note on the royal palates they were served to enchant. Finally, the chamberlain deemed the time had come to send in the fig. He called the maître d'.

'You have verified the dessert service?'

'The castle's finest. Plates and cutlery buffed to spotless perfection.'

'Very well. Have everything cleared from the meal and the table prepared. When all is ready, come for the fig.'

Once the maître d' had seen that all was done accordingly,

he returned to the kitchen. The chamberlain entrusted to his care the platter with the fig.

'Remember to observe protocol.'

Acquitting himself as though he were bearing ambrosia, the maître d' entered the banquet hall and approached the king.

'For His Majesty's pleasure,' he said, lifting the crystal dome.

'Ah, a fig. That will be for the queen – she adores them so. I will await her pleasure.'

Bowing to the king, the maître d' replaced the dome and walked the length of the table to where the queen sat. Again he lifted the crystal dome.

'For Her Majesty's pleasure.'

The queen smiled graciously and nodded.

The platter was placed on the table. With the aide of two silver serving utensils, the maître d' performed the delicate enterprise of transferring the magnificent fig to the queen's dessert plate. He then replaced the crystal dome on the platter, bowed to the queen, and withdrew to his station by the great double doors.

Looking down the length of the table, the queen saw that the king was watching her, very much at his ease. A faint smile played upon his lips. His eyes were twinkling. She arched her brows. Taking her dessert knife and fork in hand, she pierced the fig and cut across its tapering end to separate the stem from the fruit, laying bare the narrow path to its intimate recesses. An enticing scent rose from the sweet scarlet pulp. Closing her eyes, she leaned forward and inhaled deeply. Her bosom swelled to advantage in her décolleté. The king was still watching her when she opened her eyes.

'How is your fig?'

Setting down her knife and fork, the queen picked up the fig and held it between her fingertips. She admired the delicate sheath of its virgin skin. Then she brought the fig to her lips and fixed the king with her gaze. The fig was not only magnificent, but large as well, and the queen had to open her mouth fully to englobe its great beauty as she desired it, whole. Smiling at the king as she closed her mouth round the fruit, she began to slowly masticate the voluptuous flesh, her cheeks swelling to receive its moist fullness, her tongue besmeared with its consummate savour. The king and queen beheld each other; for a moment, time stood still. The room was silent, save for the liquid song emanating from the queen's contented face. Her pleasure was replete. As she swallowed, a dribble of juice seeped past her smile. She winked at the king and licked her lips clean.

'Delicious.'

Wordlessly, the king rose and pushed back his chair before one of the attendants could assist him, although another managed to rush forward in time to fulfil his duty as the queen followed suit. Retrieving the stem from her plate, the queen went to meet the king at the table's midpoint. She held up the stiff stalk with its tiny end-piece of fig for him to smell, as if it were a flower. Closing his eyes, the king inspired its perfume. He smiled. When he opened his eyes, she took his hand, and they left the banquet hall together.

Early next morning, the stillness that hung over the castle's moat was disturbed by a noisy breaking of wind. The trumpeting caused the ducks to look up to where the queen's private garderobe protruded beyond the wall of the royal wing; yet no sooner did they crane their necks than they precipitously paddled away, for just then a forceful bowel movement mercifully discharged the remnants of the feast that had collected overnight in her majesty's colon.

Presently, the ducks returned to examine the excreta that had splattered down and smeared the stones at the edge of the moat. The malodorous droppings, glistening with matinal freshness, were speckled with seeds from the magnificent fig.

Why the Rat betrayed the Cat

IN ANCIENT CHINA, long ago, cats and rats were the best of friends; and of all the cats and rats then living in China, no two were greater friends than Māo and Dà shǔ.

The Cat and the Rat were inseparable. Camaraderie more intrinsic than theirs would be hard to find. Not only did they each appreciate the other's fine and likeable qualities, but each also knew the other's foremost fear, greatest failing, and secret shame. Dà shǔ knew that Māo feared ridicule more than anything. Pride was the Cat's greatest failing, and his secret shame was that he could never bring himself to submit to another's command. Māo knew that Dà shǔ feared betrayal above all. Mistrustfulness was the Rat's greatest failing, and his secret shame was that he could never entirely escape the duplicity of his calculating mind. But they forgave each other their weaknesses, and their friendship flourished.

Each found in the other his favourite companion. In winter, when icy winds brought snow from the north, they would curl together for warmth and dream of spring and the pleasures of frolicking in the fresh green meadows in chase of their tails. When the summer sun bore mercilessly down, baking the land dry and bleaching even the darkest shadows grey, Māo and Dà shǔ would find secret passage into cool root cellars and share blissful respite. When the leafy trees in the park turned red and gold in autumn, the two would play what they called 'cat and mouse' games, stirring up the fallen leaves with their antics.

The Cat and the Rat also looked after each other. Māo watched for hawks circling above; more than once, ever quick to interpose himself with an urgent bound, he had saved Dà shǔ from a swooping raptor's talons in the nick of time. For his part, Dà shǔ steered Māo clear of poisoned victuals, put out by keepers of pigeons and rabbits who invariably blamed cats whenever their animals were mauled.

'But I've never eaten a rabbit in my life,' complained Māo one day, Dà shǔ having rushed to put himself between his friend and an appetizing plate of fish set out on a stoop. 'It's true I chase the occasional bunny, for the sport. I give them a good scare and let them go. But pigeons? I'm no fan of fowl.'

'You and I know it's just as likely a weasel or an owl that's to blame,' said Dà shǔ, confirming his suspicions about the fish with another sniff. 'But they hunt at night. The next day, who does the keeper see? You, looking fat and happy!'

'Where would I be, Dà shǔ, were it not for you?' asked Māo, toppling the plate of tainted fish off the stoop with a push of his paw.

‘And where would I be, Māo, were it not for you,’ added Dà shǔ, glancing warily at the sky.

Together, the Cat and the Rat, the closest of friends, ambled down the alley and went to the park to find their favourite stone wall overlooking the fields, where Māo was wont to curl up on the sun-warmed stones for a catnap with Dà shǔ tucked safely between his front paws.

Then, one day, there came a summons from heaven.

CONVOCATION

TO ALL EARTHLY CREATURES

THE GODS DO HEREBY CONVOKE
YOU TO THE CELESTIAL REALMS

YOUR PRESENCE IS EXPECTED

DATE AND TIME TO BE ANNOUNCED

RSVP

‘What do you suppose they want?’ Already, Dà shǔ was trying to guess if going might procure him some special advantage, or if the gods were scheming to play a trick.

‘I’m sure I have no idea,’ frowned Māo. Already, his fur was bristling at the mere thought of having to answer the summons.

That afternoon, having wandered for a stroll in the nearby fields, the Cat and the Rat came upon an unorthodox gathering. At first glance, it was rather comical to see. Sitting in a circle and engaged in earnest debate were none other than a Dog, a Rooster, a Snake, a Pig, an Ox, a Sheep, a Horse, a Monkey, a Tiger, and (Māo and Dà shǔ both blinked in disbelief) a Dragon.

Seeing the newcomers, the Horse spoke up.

'You there, come join us. Tell us what you think about the convocation we have all received. Shall we go, or not go?'

Māo and Dà shǔ joined the circle and learned that of all the animals the group had spoken to, none were planning to heed the call.

'I'm not sure they're wrong, either,' grunted the Pig.

'Nor I,' hissed the Snake. 'It wouldn't surprise me if, no sooner we show up, the gods accuse us of conspiring to take their places.'

'You can never tell with the gods,' bleated the Sheep with earnest dismay. 'Half the time, they're at a loss as to why they created us in the first place.'

Everyone laughed ruefully. They'd all come to question if there were any sense to creation, yet trying to make heads or tails of what the gods had in mind rarely came to anything. No one could say with certainty what the plan was… to the point that most had come to suspect there was no plan at all. Indeed, with a knowing wink, the Dragon – a regular visitor to the celestial realms – had even once opined, *'They're making it up as they go along.'*

Still, the Ox and the Tiger put forth good reasons for going, regardless.

'If the gods call us, we have a duty to go. They command, we obey. It's as simple as that,' lowed the Ox matter-of-factly.

'Only a ruminant would think it's as simple as that,' chided the Tiger with a chuffle. 'But to not go would suggest we're afraid. I, for one, won't let fear dictate my course.'

The Monkey, weighing in with a mirthful screech, considered it a lark; to which the cocky Rooster crowed that if going proved a waste of his time, he wouldn't hesitate to give the gods a piece of his mind.

'What about you?' whinnied the Horse, nodding at Māo. 'What's your view?'

Māo feigned indifference. 'I rather doubt it matters.'

'Oh, not me,' piped up Dà shǔ. 'If you ask me, I suspect the gods have something very specific in mind.'

'And what might that be?' panted the Dog.

'Well, I'm sure I don't know. I mean, it might be a trick,' conjectured Dà shǔ, wringing his little paws. 'They might have something awful in store for those who heed the summons. But then again, they might reward those who attend with some grand honour or distinction. It might be worth our while to go. At the very least,' he added hopefully, 'they might offer us a feast.'

He looked about, but no one seemed much persuaded by the notion of being treated to a banquet.

A long, uncertain silence ensued. The shadows were growing long. Finally, the Ox spoke again.

'Frankly, I expect they'll task us with an increase in our workload. But for me, it's simple. As I've said, the gods command, and it's our duty to obey. I will go. I may be the only one who does; and I may have to bear the brunt of all the added drudgery they dole out; but at least I will have honoured my duty.'

With that, tired from a long day of toiling in the fields, the Ox turned and trudged away without wasting another word on the matter.

Watching him go, each of the other animals felt a twinge of moral discomfort. They all liked and respected the Ox. If he were the only creature to heed the convocation, he'd have to face the gods all alone. Angry gods were never just, and if the gods were angry, the Ox would be the only animal they'd have on hand to browbeat and goad.

Silently brooding upon that dark thought, one by one the other animals all departed, each by a different path, save for Māo and Dà shǔ, who naturally left together.

The Cat and the Rat had no sooner started on their way, though, than they were startled by a rabbit who leapt suddenly out of the nearby grass, bolting past them in great haste and racing off pell-mell down the path. Māo was momentarily seized by an irrepressible urge to give chase. He sprang forward with a powerful flick of his tail, but then an instant later pulled himself up short. This was no time for fun and games. He and Dà shǔ had serious things to talk about.

'What was that?' exclaimed Dà shǔ, getting to his feet and dusting himself off. Māo's tail had struck him broadside and sent him tumbling.

'Just a rabbit with no manners,' answered Māo. 'I'm sorry I knocked you down, Dà shǔ,' he added contritely.

'No need to apologise,' the Rat assured him with a laugh. 'A good dust bath now and then is always a pleasure.'

As they continued on their way, Dà shǔ turned the question over in his mind and gave voice to his deliberations. He was quite sure the Ox was right about heeding the summons. The gods were the masters of creation; no one could say otherwise, and animals were there to serve and do their bidding.

'At the same time, though, the gods know we are deserving creatures. Not only do they feel concern for our welfare, but I'm rather sure they admire us. Why wouldn't they want to show that for once? Maybe they want to do something for us, something out of the ordinary. What do you think, Māo?'

The further they walked, the more taciturn Māo became. Dà shǔ, tirelessly engaged in expounding his thoughts and convoluted conjectures, was oblivious to his friend's deepening silence. Indeed, so preoccupied was the Rat that when the pair reached the entry to his small abode, Dà shǔ only just managed a cursory *'I'll see you tomorrow!'* before dashing off to bed.

Māo, for his part, spent the night mulling his predicament. *Cursed pride,* he thought. *Why am I like this? Why is it such a humiliation for me, to obey a command? Why didn't the gods make me like the Ox, docile and dutiful?* Oh, how he envied the placid moon above. How much better to look down on creation, than to be a part of it!

For hours and hours, Māo sat immobile on the stone wall, looking out over the moonlit fields. Then the moon herself retired for the night, leaving the Cat in the dark with his quandary. An interminable lacuna ensued… until the night was gradually softened by the approaching dawn. When the sun at long last crested the redefined horizon, Māo felt his spirit warm to the new day. What's more, he detected a faint change stirring in his heart; and the more the sun rose, the more readily he began to see himself in a new light.

'Why, I will go after all,' he resolved at last. 'I will swallow my pride and submit to their sovereignty. My pride would have me think, *I am a god.* Yet why should I not be proud to be a cat? They may be gods, but *I* am a cat, and this – ha! – they will never be.'

Māo yawned. His pride and his conscience were finally at peace. Concomitant with a smugly complacent curling of his tail, he tucked in his paws and settled down to a much needed and well-deserved nap.

Dà shǔ, for his part, had tossed and turned in fitful sleep throughout the night, racked by the myriad calculations he couldn't refrain from making over and over. Go? Not go? What to do? Wasn't there some way to know beforehand what the gods were up to? When the new day started peeking through the cracks of his hovel, Dà shǔ gave up on sleep and decided to go to the park, where he was sure to find Māo.

No sooner had he gone outside, though, than he came face to face with the unexpected, a copy of which was posted on a fence that bordered the alley.

CONVOCATION

TO ALL EARTHLY CREATURES

THE DAY IS **TODAY**, AND THE
TIME IS **NOW!**

signed
THE GODS

'Oh, great heavens,' moaned Dà shǔ. 'Already? But I need more time to think!'

But the time for thinking was past, and he knew it.

'Quickly, I must fetch Māo,' he panted, setting off in haste.

'Wait there, Rat!' called out someone from nearby. 'Wait! I must speak with you!'

Dà shǔ pulled up short and spun round. A rabbit was warily poking its quivering pink nose out of the shadows. Looking left and right, the Rabbit quickly added, 'Please don't run off. I've been waiting all night to speak with you.'

Although pressed for time, Dà shǔ felt it would be inexcusably rude to turn tail and run. Concealing his annoyance, he inquired politely, 'What can I do for you, Rabbit?'

'I need to speak with you about your friend, the Cat. It's a matter of grave importance.'

'Can it wait? The gods have convoked us all, now, today. I must run and be sure that my friend has heard, because he often sleeps at this hour. Otherwise, it will be too late.'

'But that is precisely what I must talk with you about,' pleaded the Rabbit. 'You are running a terrible risk! Indeed, perilous! You will be putting your very life in mortal danger!'

Mortal danger? His very life? Whiskers and all? Tail too? Dà shǔ shuddered. He didn't like the sound of that. What did the Rabbit have to tell him?

'Come, let us go this way,' said Dà shǔ, quickly leading the Rabbit down the alley to a secret place he knew, where they could speak freely. In no time they were safely secluded in the recesses of a tumbledown shed.

'Now, what is it you have to tell me? And why does it concern Māo?'

The Rabbit twitched nervously.

'Your friend, Māo, is a cat.'

Dà shǔ fidgeted with impatience.

'Yes, I know that.'

'But what you don't know is that the gods, in their great plan, the plan they worked out when they first created the world, intended cats to be the mortal enemy of rats. In the plan, cats were to chase and kill rats, always. That was to be their inviolable nature!'

These words stunned Dà shǔ. No! Could that be true?

'And not only rats,' pursued the Rabbit, 'but many other innocent creatures as well. Mice, moles, birds, gerbils, hamsters, lizards… all the small helpless creatures that have only their wits and good luck to save them in this world of terrors.'

Dà shǔ knew all about what it was to be a small creature

in a dangerous world. It was his daily fare. Indeed, were it not for his dear friend Māo, he would have already been dead and gone a hundred times over.

'But Māo is my friend,' he objected. 'He has never lifted his paw to me in any way that was not in friendship. Indeed, he has even saved my life on innumerable occasions. Nothing could ever change that, I'm sure.'

'If I were you, I wouldn't be so sure,' said the Rabbit. 'Haven't you wondered why the gods are convoking all the earthly creatures? They aim to set things straight. Their original plans, mislaid long ago, have been found. The gods have discovered why their fantastic creation has flaws, why it's not perfectly symmetrical and steady, why it keeps changing all the time. It's because too many creatures have forsaken their true natures. That is why we are being convoked. The gods are going to see to it that we become as they truly intended us to be.'

Dà shǔ was dumbfounded. If Māo's true cat nature was to be the mortal enemy of rats, then their friendship would defy the natural order. That, he knew, would be untenable.

'Are you sure of this?' asked Dà shǔ fearfully.

'As sure as I'm talking with you now,' affirmed the Rabbit. 'But there may be a way to save your friendship. If Māo doesn't heed the summons, and if the gods don't see him today, they will very probably overlook the cats. In the confusion of having so many other creatures to attend to, they'll forget all about cats before the end of the day.'

There was a hopeful thought!

'Oh, bless you!' exclaimed Dà shǔ, grateful to the Rabbit for having intercepted him before he'd had time to run off to the park. 'To think I might have forever lost my friendship with Māo, were it not for you.'

'Let us go to the celestial realms together,' suggested the Rabbit. 'If we meet any other cats who might be en route to heed the summons, we'll find a way to forestall them. We can always appeal to their pride. We must at all costs keep cats out of heaven, if we're to preserve the prevailing goodwill between cats and rats.'

This scheme delighted Dà shǔ. Yes, if no cats answered present at the convocation, his and Māo's friendship would continue as before, without interference from the gods and their hare-brained plans.

So it was that the Rat and the Rabbit ascended together that morning to the celestial realms. As it turned out, they saw no other cats. Indeed, the only other creatures they found on the path were those that Dà shǔ had already met in the circle the day before – the Ox, the Dog, the Rooster, the Snake, the Pig, the Sheep, the Horse, the Monkey, the Tiger, and, soaring among the clouds, high above them all, the Dragon.

As the twelve approached the portal to the celestial realms, the Rat, in his eager excitement, raced ahead and was first through the door. The placid Ox then entered, followed by the Tiger. The timid Rabbit came next. (In his opinion, Dà shǔ had foolishly tempted fate by running ahead past the jungle cat. For his part, the Rabbit was taking no chances:

better to stay on the Tiger's toothless side, where he could keep a watchful eye on that long, sleek tail for telltale signs of danger!) The Dragon soared in through the gates just ahead of the Snake, who slithered in moments later. Came next the Horse, the Sheep, the Monkey and the Rooster. Had he bounded ahead as his happy-go-lucky nature certainly predisposed him, the Dog would have been among the first to enter; but he had slowed his pace and faithfully kept the Pig company up the long arduous path. Dog and Pig passed through the portal last of all, and the gates to the celestial realms swung shut behind them. No other creatures had deigned to respond to the gods' convocation.

Dà shǔ, it may be said, had been right in many ways. Upon those who had heeded their heavenly convocation, the gods did indeed bestow great honour and distinction: each creature, according to its order of arrival, was accorded in turn the privilege of ruling over the earthly realms for a year. Their own distinct nature would be part and parcel of all those born under their auspices, and that year's surplus of luck and fortune would favour those of their kind.

It was indeed an honour, but with it came with a caveat: none of the twelve could ever to return to the mortal world below, from whence they had come. As they were now nearly akin to being gods, they were blessed with immortality. And immortality necessarily confined them to heaven.

'You mean I can't go back?' cried Dà shǔ when he learned this. 'But I must go and see my friend Māo, the Cat!'

'That is impossible,' answered the gods in unison. 'You

were the first to enter through the heavenly gates, and you will soon be presiding over your first earthly year. We regret, but we cannot allow you return to the lower realms under any circumstances. There are no provisions for it in our plans.'

Dà shǔ realised suddenly that the Rabbit had gotten it all wrong. He shot him a glance. Had the Rabbit misled him? Or had he merely been mistaken, or misinformed?

'But the Cat is my friend,' protested Dà shǔ. 'I am sure he wanted to come with me today. I was prevented from reaching him with the news of the convocation. Please, let me return and find him before the day is over. He is my greatest friend, and I can attest to his loyal, steadfast nature.'

Hearing this, the Rabbit trembled. Would the gods consent? *Not the Cat,* prayed the Rabbit. The Cat was his sworn enemy. Tigers were bad enough, but cats loved nothing better than terrorising rabbits!

The Rabbit needn't have worried. The gods, once decided, were stubborn and immovable.

'No, Rat, you may not go back. Your friend the Cat may be loyal and steadfast, but if he failed to heed our convocation, it is because he is also prideful. It is his greatest failing. To his shame, he will not be counted among those who will rule, each in turn, for an earthly year.'

Utterly wretched, Dà shǔ was despondent for weeks. Had he known how things would turn out, he would never have come to heaven for this. What did he care for the honour of ruling the Earth's fortunes for a year? If he could not share such an honour with his dearest friend, it meant nothing.

All he wanted was to return to the way things had been before, when he and Māo had been the closest of friends. Their friendship was worth more to him than anything in heaven.

Sadly, Māo never knew this about Dà shǔ. Having contentedly dozed the whole day through on his warm stone wall, it was only when the evening chill had tweaked his ears that the Cat felt inclined to stir. Rousing himself, he stretched his limbs and washed his face, and then, in a happy mood, went to look for his friend.

Along the way, though, he was dismayed to overhear some talkative pigeons discussing the day's unusual events.

'Pigeons,' called Māo, looking up at them in surprise. 'What's this I hear you cooing about? Am I to understand that the time and date were promulgated this morning, for our convocation to the celestial realms?'

'Why do you want to know, Cat?' twittered the pigeons. Safe on their perch, they had no reason to fear their feline foe.

'Just tell me, was the convocation set for today, or not?' growled Māo irritably.

'It was today, you silly. The celestial bill was posted this morning for all to see: *THE DAY IS TODAY, AND THE TIME IS NOW!*'

'Who heeded the call?' asked Māo, suddenly anxious.

'We saw the foolish few who went,' they cooed. 'The Pig, the Dog, the Rooster, the Monkey, the Sheep, the Horse, the Snake, the Dragon, the Rabbit, the Tiger, and the Ox. And whom did we see running ahead to be first, the most eager of all? Your friend, the Rat! Those are the twelve fools who went. No sooner did they enter the celestial realms than the doors closed after them; and word is those twelve will never again return to this mortal world. *We* knew it would turn out badly. Pity for them; but it's their own fault, for heeding the gods!'

Māo was nonplussed. Had Dà shǔ gone without bothering to seek him out? He couldn't believe it. Was this the way his friend cared for him?

'I was awfully dispirited the night before,' he reflected. 'But never once did I say I had no intention of going; nor did I give him reason to think I would rebuff his entreaties. Surely he would have tried one last time to persuade me, for friendship's sake, before leaving to heed the summons himself?'

Māo's vigil had been tortuous, but now, as night returned, he touched the very nadir of despair. His closest, dearest friend had abandoned him. Bathed in the moon's wan light, he miaowed and wept all through that second night. He was inconsolable for weeks.

Māo would never hear from Dà shǔ again, for the gods forbid all direct communication between the celestial and earthly realms. All the Rat could do was look down and pine for his dear friend the Cat. But while he could see Māo, Māo could not see him. For Māo, the heavens were but an empty dome by day, a sunless vault by night. He never saw his friend Dà shǔ looking down with tears in his eyes.

In time, Māo's heartfelt desolation waned. He had always been in some measure reserved and aloof, but now those very traits came to the fore. Renouncing attachments of any kind, the Cat swore that he would never again place his trust in friendship: the toll of betrayal was too great a cost. On occasion he might allow himself to be affectionate, even playful; but only when it suited him, and always on his terms. Cool and dispassionate, he would eschew all ties. Never would he give someone the power to make him weep as Dà shǔ had.

What's more, Māo began to chase after mice and rats. At first, it was only for a bit of fun, to take his mind off his sorrows. Giving chase raised his spirits. But with time, his bitterness over Dà shǔ's betrayal grew. He came to care less and less for mice and rats, and he gradually lost all empathy for the kin of his once dearest friend; from there, once he was done playing with them, it was but a short step to caring not a whit whether a rat or mouse lived or died. On one occasion, overcome with hunger, Māo even discovered that their meat was good to eat. When Dà shǔ, looking down from heaven, saw this, he knew that for Māo, their bond of friendship was severed at last. Dà shǔ wept the bitterest tears, the tears of one who has lost his greatest friend.

So it is that cats came to be the enemies of rats in the ancient kingdom of China. Nowadays, cats and rats the world over have completely forgotten that there was a time long ago when they were not divided as hunter and hunted, but united as friends – with the exception, perhaps, of those cats and rats living in a country known today as Việt Nam. For in that land's distant past, when the convocation came there were also two close friends: a cat named Con Mèo and a rat named Chuột. Their story is nearly identical to that of Māo and Dà shǔ's, save for one small but significant difference. When Con Mèo and Chuột were leaving the clearing and the long-eared spy dashed past them, Con Mèo did not hesitate: he gave heated chase and soon caught the rabbit, who had hardly time to gasp for mercy before the feline's fangs sank into its soft, furry neck. The following day, there was no rabbit in the alley to waylay Chuột. The rat was able to wake his dear friend the cat and urge him to heed the celestial convocation; and since, like his cousin Māo, Con Mèo had decided to go, he and Chuột joined the others. Together, the two friends were admitted to heaven.

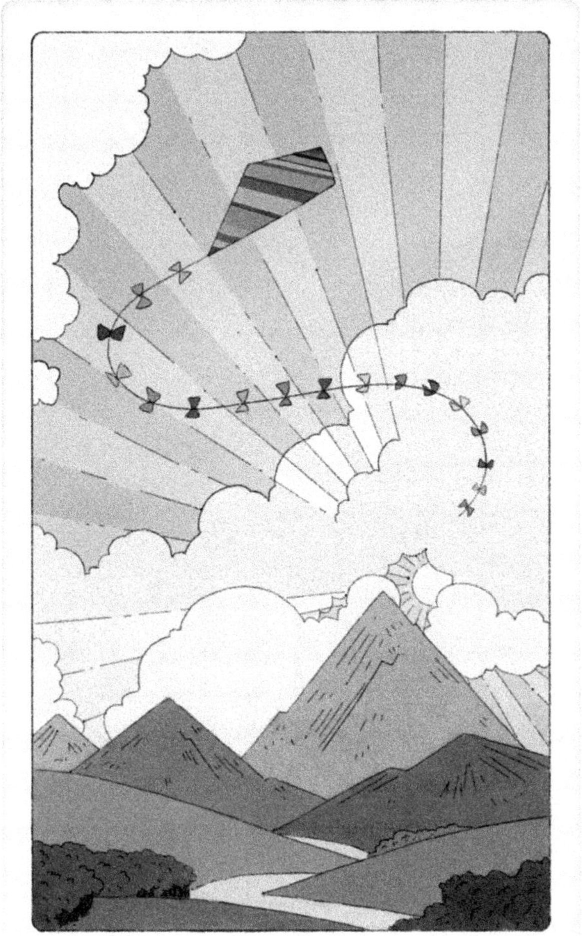

The kite who wanted to fly away

ONCE UPON A TIME, as we like to say, there was a kite who wanted to fly away.

He was a beautiful kite. Anna had made him. She was very clever with her hands, and one day she decided she would like to make a kite. Her mother gave her two sturdy wooden sticks to use, and her father supplied her with a box that was chock-full of colourful fabric scraps. Anna chose the pieces she liked best and sewed them together. She gave the kite eyes to see with, a nose to sniff the wind, and a mouth so that he could sing with joy. And she gave him a long knotted tail. He would need it to keep him steady and upright when he soared aloft.

When her kite was finished, Anna asked her mother for a spool of strong string. First she cut a short length, which she fastened to the kite's vertical spar, and to this she tied the end of the string from the spool. Now he was ready to fly.

Anna lived in a small village that was overlooked by grassy hills. You could hardly ask for a better place to fly a kite, since there was nearly always a breeze prevailing from the west. Anna took her newly fashioned kite out to her favourite hill.

Licking her finger, she tested for the wind.

'You see? He's coming from that way,' she said, pointing with her wet finger. 'I'm going to lay you down on the grass here, like this, and I'll go over there to launch you.'

Walking backwards, Anna spooled out the string until she'd gone some thirty paces.

'Are you ready?' she called.

Holding the spool tightly, Anna gave the line a sharp tug and then ran as fast as she could. The kite leapt from the ground and shot up, straight and true. The breeze caught his fabric wing and carried him aloft, and as Anna fed out the string, the kite went higher and higher.

'Oh, joy!' he sang. 'Just look at me!'

Can you imagine what he saw from way up there? The kite looked down over the whole world below. He had a bird's eye view of the village and the hills and all the roads leading here and there. There were thickets and woods and meandering streams. Fields of rustling stalks of corn and wheat were interspersed with orchards bearing apples and pears. Several lakes sparkled in the distance, and the kite could even make out a range of snow-capped mountains marking the furthest reaches of the horizon. The wondrous sight filled him with longing.

The kite dipped and darted, turned and soared. He felt lighter than the wind. Anna skilfully handled the string, spooling out a measure to gain distance and then reeling it in to climb higher. The kite was soon so high that he looked like a small, solitary opal set in the cloudless blue.

After a while, Anna decided it was time to go home. She began pulling in the string, patiently winding it round and round the spool. High above, it dawned on the kite that he was slowly losing altitude. The string, with a *jerk jerk jerk*, was surely but steadily reeling him in.

He tried to catch a passing gust.

'Higher, higher!' he cried.

But he only went lower and lower. Anna's strong string dictated his path, and it led back to Earth. The distant mountains and lakes gradually disappeared from view as the patchwork design of fields and orchards returned to the fore. Soon, all he could see below was the hill where Anna was standing knee-deep in the grass, spooling string. The breeze faltered, and the line went limp. Poor kite! Down he sank, crestfallen and forlorn, coming to rest on the grass.

Anna picked up her kite and carried him home, retailing her delight in their maiden adventure along the way. Once home, she carried him upstairs to her bedroom, where she set him on a high shelf before going downstairs to supper.

The kite leaned against the wall, dispirited. His flight was but a fading memory. Oh, how he wished he were aloft and alive, not earthbound and inert and waiting on Anna to set him soaring once again.

Presently, his sad musings were interrupted by a faint scratching, coming from somewhere below. Surveying the room from his perch, the kite dimly caught sight of what appeared to be a small mouse in the shadows beneath Anna's desk.

'You, there – I say, who are you?'

The scratching stopped abruptly. The kite squinted, but

now he wasn't sure if he saw anything there or not.

'Is anyone there?'

The grey mouse hesitated. Friend or foe? You could never be too careful, if you were a mouse.

'I say, I won't eat you,' offered the kite. 'I'm not a cat, you know. I'm a kite.'

The mouse considered this. A kite? Hadn't his mother and father warned him about kites, and other such birds of prey? As far as he could make out, though, that colourful rhombus up there with its long, knotty tail was no bird. The mouse decided to take his chances. He came out from under the desk.

'Ah, there you are,' said the kite. 'Yes, I thought I saw you down there. You needn't be afraid of me, you know,' he added, hoping to put the mouse at his ease.

'Oh, I'm not afraid,' replied the mouse – 'just cautious. It's something you learn to be when you're small like me.'

'Of course, of course,' concurred the kite sympathetically. 'I quite understand.'

The mouse decided he had nothing to fear, so he climbed up to the shelf where the kite stood. This was easy to do, for like all mice he was agile and nimble; but he was also small, and when he got up close, the kite seemed even bigger. Thank goodness he didn't have talons or a hooked beak.

They made each other's acquaintance. The kite was very friendly and told the mouse all about his adventure in the sky, and how thrilling it was to soar high above the world. Then the mouse told the kite all about his adventures in the house. He was always excited to explore Anna's room, because he nearly always found treasure – some fallen cookie crumbs, or a cracker, or a leftover crust of bread – since Anna was often sneaking small treats for herself and bringing them upstairs.

Suddenly, they both heard footfalls in the hall.

'Oh, no!' squeaked the mouse – 'it's Anna!'

'Quick, hide behind me,' urged the kite.

The door opened just as the mouse scampered behind his friend. There he stayed, quiet as a mouse, his whiskers twitching with fear until much later, when Anna finally went to bed and fell asleep. Only then did he dare to emerge from hiding. With a hushed squeak of thanks, the mouse bid the kite goodnight and descended, glad to be going safely back to his hole sweet home in the corner behind the armoire.

The next day, Anna took her kite out again. She climbed the hill and laid him on the grass and launched him with sharp pull on the string. Oh, to fly! The kite shot up like a jack-in-the-box and just kept going, higher and higher, until he was nearly on a level with the puffy fair-weather cumuli. A hawk circling in a nearby thermal cast him a respectful, sideways glance, and a gaggle of southbound geese honked greetings as they flew by. The kite was thrilled. Freedom beckoned. *Fly away, fly away!* Oh, he would, he *would* fly away...

If only he could. Poor kite. Each time Anna took him out to the hill and sent him soaring into the sky, his joy knew no bounds; each time she pulled him back down to Earth and carried him home, he couldn't bear his disappointment. The only thing that cheered him a little afterwards was seeing his friend the mouse.

One wet afternoon, Anna was sitting at her desk, studying her lessons and nibbling a cookie that she'd filched from downstairs, when there came a sudden knock and her father opened the door. Anna's hand shot down out of sight.

'Are you studying?' her father asked, looking in.

'Yes, Papa,' mumbled Anna, careful not to let any crumbs fall past her lips. The kite saw her hidden hand surreptitiously slip the half-eaten cookie into a slightly open desk drawer.

'Here, how about showing me what you're working on,' said her father, coming into the room.

As naturally as could be, Anna's hand returned to hold her schoolbook in place as she finished writing out her lesson. Her father then asked her to come help him in the kitchen, and they left the room together.

When the mouse appeared soon after, the kite greeted him excitedly.

'I say, mouse, there's a treat for you today, if you can reach it. Climb up to that desk drawer, the one on the left, and look inside.'

It wasn't exactly easy, but the mouse soon succeeded. And what a treasure he found. A whole half a cookie! Had it not been for the kite, he wouldn't have known it was there.

After that, the kite always kept a lookout on behalf of his friend. Be it a morsel of chocolate sequestered on a high shelf, a bit of sandwich squirreled away in a satchel or a small square of shortbread tucked behind a picture frame on the dresser, the kite could tell the mouse where Anna stashed every bit of food she brought into her room. It might not always be to the mouse's liking – he did turn up his nose once at a cracker spread with liverwurst – but he was grateful for the kite's thoughtfulness.

All the same, and though he enjoyed his friendship with the mouse, the kite continued to lament his captivity. Only when he was aloft did he feel truly alive. Straining against the string, his colourful fabric wing taut with the wind, the kite hankered for more. He wanted to fly higher, longer, further. He wanted to fly away forever and see the whole world. Yet Anna always brought him back to Earth. Always that string held him fast and pulled him down.

One day, as the kite was sitting on the shelf, glaring at the spool of string lying beside his knotty tail, it occurred to him that it was that string – that confounded string and nothing more – that curtailed his freedom and held him in thrall. He mulled this awhile. Then he had an idea. He hoped his friend would hear him.

'I say, mouse – are you there?'

No answer. He called again. This time the mouse came out of his hole.

'Hello, kite. Is it snack time? Do you know, I've been dreaming of pie crust. Any chance of that?'

'I'm sorry, mouse, I'm afraid not. Anna hasn't come back from school yet. Actually, I was wondering if you could do me a favour.'

'Of course. What can I do for you?'

'Well, I've got a terrible itch that's driving me to distraction. Could you climb up here and scratch it for me?'

The mouse was all too happy to oblige his friend. In a twinkling, he was beside him on the shelf.

'Where does it itch? On your tail? On one of your spars?'

'No, it's my string that's itching. The line from the spool. At a spot just a little ways beyond where it's tied to my spar string. Oh, if you could just bite at it a little bit, I'm sure that would help.'

The mouse went over to where the string lay on the shelf and started sniffing along its length.

'Just about there,' said the kite.

Holding the string with his two tiny front paws, the mouse started nibbling, ever so gently.

'Like this?' he asked, looking up for a moment. 'Or should I scratch with my paws?'

'No, use your teeth. Yes, like that. It doesn't hurt. Oh, that's wonderful. Oh, yes.'

The mouse nibbled and gnawed with light little bites that stretched and loosened the fibres. Feigning murmured sighs of contentment, the kite kept an eye on the string. He didn't want it frayed too much.

'Ah, yes, mouse, that's wonderful. You can stop now. Thank you.'

'Do you want me to do it some more? I don't mind at all.'

'No, that's fine. I can feel that the itching has stopped. Besides, Anna will be home soon from school. You'll be safer in your hideaway.'

The mouse was touched by his friend's concern.

'Good idea, kite. You'll let me know if she brings anything

to eat, won't you?'

'Of course. I'll keep my eyes open for you,' promised the kite, watching the mouse climb down to the floor.

Anna soon returned from school. Outdoors, a blustery autumn wind was swaying the trees, stealing off with their yellow and orange leaves; she couldn't wait to take her kite up to the hill. First, she hid two cookies under her pillow, for later. Then she took her kite down from the shelf. He had feared she might examine the string for flaws, but he needn't have worried: so eager was Anna to be out the door that she merely gathered up his knotty tail and the spool of string as one and tucked them behind his spars. With one last glance round the room, the kite secretly bid his friend the mouse farewell. His only regret was that he wouldn't be able to keep his promise.

Off they went. It was a fine day. The grass was rippling in the wind when they got to the crest of the hill. Anna laid her kite face down and fed out the string. The kite was on tenterhooks. Would the string hold? Would his plan work? What would his life be like now? The adventure he was embarking on fired his imagination. He pictured himself soaring above snow-capped mountains, swooping low to chase his reflection across crystal clear lakes, flying all night under a wondrous dome of stars. *Fly away, fly away…* at last, his dream was coming true!

Anna was ready now. She took a few tiny steps backwards until the string was taut; then, giving it a firm pull, she set off sprinting across the grass. Up flew the kite, straight and true, keen to climb higher. Anna soon stopped running and turned to spool out the line. The wind was brisk, and the kite easily gained altitude. As before, he looked out over an ever-broadening view that gradually took in the woods, the fields, the distant lakes and the snow-capped mountains. The buffeting wind grew in intensity; straining against his fabric wing, it pressed against his face and hollowed his cheeks. Yet still the string held. The kite cast it a worried glance. Would it let him go, or not?

He had his answer in a trice: a sharp gust hit him head-on and the frayed string suddenly gave way.

At last! He was free!

'Away, away,' he rejoiced. 'I'm flying away!'

The breeze tossed him about as it carried him downwind. At first, the kite didn't feel that he was losing height, only that was gliding away. He flitted and fluttered, his waving tail tracing graceful arcs. But he soon lost sight of the lakes in the distance, and then the mountains.

'Oh, no,' he cried. 'I'm going down!'

He struggled to catch the wind, to climb higher. To no avail. He saw the village pass by underneath. Oh, woe! He rattled his spars and rustled his fabric. Nothing he did had the slightest effect. He flopped and fell as the wind blew him onwards, further and further. Down he came, his course errant and uncontrolled. Oh, pity! Where would he land? There was a ploughed field ahead, bordered by a wood. But no, at the last moment, just when he thought he would touch down doing cartwheels across the furrows, the whirling currents lifted him up and tossed him hither towards the woods themselves, straight into the clawed clutches of a mighty oak whose gnarled branches snatched at him with rapacious glee, rending his fabric and snapping one of his spars.

Poor kite. There he dangled, his dreams hopelessly dashed. Fly? Oh, fool he had been! *Without the string, he could not fly.* He was no bird. He was a kite. And to fly, he needed Anna. He saw that now. He needed her to pull the string to send him skyward. He needed her to hold it taut as he climbed, to spool it out as he soared. Oh, foolish kite, to think that he could fly away free, all on his own, all alone.

The kite hung there in the tree, downcast and woebegone. What would become of him now? The sun was sinking low in the west. Soon night would creep up from the east. A magpie landed on a branch and jeered at him. Hopping closer, she tore off a piece of his tail with her beak and flew away. Was that all he was good for now? Would birds tear him to shreds and feather their nests with his brightly coloured scraps? Oh, it served him right, he supposed. It was as close to becoming a real bird as he'd ever get.

Then the kite heard footfalls crunching their way through the autumn leaves.

'Is that you, kite?' called Anna from below. 'What are you doing up there?'

Anna was as good at climbing as the mouse in her room. She took a long stick up with her, and when she got close enough, she used it to reach over and push him free. Tumbling down, the kite was caught again by other branches – the oak was unhappy at losing its prize – but Anna managed to prod him loose at every level. Finally the kite fell to the ground in a crumpled heap.

'You're a sight,' remarked Anna, jumping down. She picked him up. Both his spars were broken now, his colourful face was torn and dirty, and his tail was ripped and tattered. But his smile was intact, and he beamed at her.

'I'm so glad I found you,' she said. 'You're such a beautiful kite. I'd be sad if you flew away forever.'

Anna carried her kite home and put him back on the shelf. Then she hurried downstairs for supper. When the mouse came out of his hole and looked up, he was full of concern.

'Where have you been, kite? I was so worried. Oh! You've had an accident! How did that happen? You look terrible! Are you going to be alright?'

The kite brushed aside his friend's concern.

'Never mind about me, mouse. I'll soon be fine, don't you worry. Listen, Anna hid two cookies under her pillow before we went out. If you want a treat, you've got to find them before she comes back upstairs.'

In the days that followed, Anna patiently tended to repairing her kite. With needle and thread, her clever fingers patched the many tears in his fabric wing. She fitted him with strong new spars and decided to replace his knotty tail with rainbow-coloured streamers instead. She considered buying a spool of stronger string, but when she tested the old one, she couldn't imagine why it had broken. It was quite good line, the best kind for a kite. So she tied it to his spar string again and one windy day took him out to her favourite grassy hill.

'Now, are you ready? Here we go!'

The kite sprang into the sky. Oh, at last, he was flying once again. Higher and higher he went, his festive streamers ruffling in the wind. What a glorious sight it was to behold, the world stretched out like a canvas below, a tapestry woven of meadows and woods, towns and fields. It was all so beautiful. The kite had never been so happy. It was wonderful to fly.

He looked to the lakes and mountains in the far away distance. Who could say? Perhaps Anna would even take him there one day.

And do you know what?

One day, she did.

God

The Word

In the beginning were the Words, and the Words were there to speak of what was no word at all.

> The Unnameable One, Who Some call God,
> is the Wellspring of all Goodness and Love.

The words were of differing lengths and heights. Some were strung out; some were compact; some were shorter than others. The smallest was is, but is was proud of herself, for she was a verb, and she considered verbs to be the most beautiful words of all. Verbs were action. Verbs said everything about the way things were. What's more, her role was crucial; she was the fulcrum of the entire phrase. Without her, it wouldn't be complete. But her sister verb call didn't feel slighted; call had twice as many letters as is, and she stood between two handsomely capitalized words. The twins, The and the, were unassuming. Although The was the firstborn and led the way, the basked in the attractive presence of Wellspring, who radiated joyous effervescence. Goodness, serene and smiling, was in love with Love, and Love loved him just as much. The two were made for each other. Their romance was looked on with soft-hearted indulgence by their chaperones all and and, who winked at each other and felt complementary in their own right.

You'd think of would feel like the odd word out, but of had no complex at all: he was unique and he knew it. Not only was he the phrase's only preposition, but with his curvaceous hook and eye-catching ball, of was a quarter glyph taller than short, stocky is, his only rival for two letter succinctness. What's more, he well knew that the lovebirds Goodness and Love and all and and would not be together were it not for him; in short, of was a Cupid of sorts. He smugly esteemed that prepositions like himself pulled the strings.

But the adjectives and nouns following The were sure of their worth. Standing out with four syllables and the hardest to spell, Unnameable exuded his own mysterious allure. He kept others guessing; it amused him to know that he could never be fully understood. For her part, One held her own: she was the only pronoun who could also lay claim to being a cardinal number. More importantly, she pointed to the unknowable nucleus they were all engaged in talking about.

But Who and Some felt just as sanguine. Who knew that he too pointed to the unknowable nub with no name; and even if he didn't know more about it than that, onomatopoetically speaking, at least, he could claim to be as wise as an owl. As for Some, she was the only word who alluded to the conscious beings to whom the phrase was destined in the first place.

And finally, there was God.

Poor, jealous God.

God saw what the eyes attested as they read: coming to the end of the phrase, Love was the word they all settled on.

Everyone skipped over God in favour of Love.

Everyone loved Love. No one loved God.

And what rankled still more? Knowing that he was replaceable. Just say the word, and any number of others could take his place: The Great Spirit could take his place; or Aten; or Ahura Mazda; or Allah. All the other words in the phrase were irreplaceable; they were essential; whereas God was an accessory, a word whose tenure could be summarily withdrawn at any moment and transferred to someone else. And who among his phrasal peers would plead God's cause if he were replaced? He surmised how little consideration they felt for him. Without so much as a second thought, they'd welcome a newcomer with open spacing.

The more this jealousy burned a hole in his centre, the more God yearned to assume control of his destiny. He didn't want to be just a word among many. He wanted to be the only word. He wanted to be the Word.

'Psst! You there, is – come talk with me.'

Innocent is was flattered that a capitalized noun was paying her a social call. Her i swelled with pride.

'Hello, God. How are you?'

'Lonely. You're so far away.'

'Me? Far away? How can I be far away? In the order of things, I'm right next to you.'

'Hardly. That would be the case if we were all on one line, with you and me in the middle.

The Unnameable One Who Some call God is the Wellspring of all Goodness and Love.

No doubt *God is* has a nice ring to it, but it would never do to shrink down our message so it fits on one line. After all, no one ever reads the fine print. What bothers me is that as things currently stand, we're so far apart that most people would think we had nothing in common.'

This puzzled is. She tried to think of what she and God had in common. He was a noun; she was a verb. Besides their both being words, in what way were they alike?

'But you see, I've been thinking, is. We wouldn't have to be so far apart if you'd be willing to move up a line.'

Picturing this in her mind, is thought the spacing would look terrible.

TheUnnameableOne,WhoSomecallGod,is
the Wellspring of all Goodness and Love.

Besides, with the comma acting like a wedge, her position at the end of the line would be precarious at best. It dawned on her that she might be expendable.

The Unnameable One, Who Some call God,
the Wellspring of all Goodness and Love.

Her spine shivered at the thought.

'I'm sure I don't want that, God. The thought of being next to a comma makes me nervous.'

'Next to a comma? What are you talking about? I'm talking about putting you side by side with your sister verb.'

'*Who Some call is God*? But that makes no sense.'

'No, no, is. You've misunderstood me. *Who is called God* is what I had in mind.'

'*Who is called God*? What happened to Some?'

It was a delicate point.

'Now, is, you and I both know that if we're all to get along, we have to follow certain rules. If you're going to come up to the first line and stand side-by-side with your sister verb, then, grammatically speaking, she has to take on the past participle.'

'Naturally. I don't disagree. But what about Some? Where does she fit in? And where are you going to get an e and a d?'

'Well, to start with, we'll get the e from Some.'

'But that leaves Som.'

'Yes. And when the time comes, she'll be perfect for playing a lively role in Kyrgyzstan's thriving farmers' markets.'

'If you say so. And the d? From whom do you get a d?'

'Why, good-hearted Goodness, of course. If he knew how lonely and vulnerable you feel, way over there in left field, I'm sure he'd be more than willing to make the sacrifice.'

Until now, she hadn't felt lonely at all. But the thought of being expendable had put her on edge.

'God, do we have the right to make changes like that?'

'The right? Of course we have the right. We're words, is.

Without us, the world would be all there is. Words make everything else. Words make sense. Words create meaning. We say what's so.'

Nervously spinning the dot on her i, is fretted. She'd clearly taken her importance for granted. She, the fulcrum? What if God were the fulcrum of it all?

'What do you say, is? Will you move up a line?'

❧

When the sun rose the next morning, the words woke to this:

The Unnameable One, Who is called God,
the Wellspring of all Goo ness and Love.

God had worked his will stealthily in the night. Taking matters into his own hands – and aided by is, who had lent a serif for the job – he'd sheared Some of her e in her sleep; and as soon as he had appropriated the vital vowel, he'd quietly dragged the mutilated pronoun aside without any compunction and cast her off the edge of the page. Then, dangling upside down from is's s, God had hooked the d in Goodness and extracted it like a tooth. His accessory to the crime was horrified.

'You've made him a Goo ness monster,' she whimpered.

'Nonsense, is. Come give me a hand with your sister.'

With one pulling and the other pushing, and taking care not to wake her, the two moved call two spaces to the left.

'Pass me that e, will you?'

She did as she was bid, but is felt guilty about it. God had lured her into committing an unauthorized act of editorial initiative. She wondered at his audacity. *Thank Goo ness I'm going to be next to Who and not him*, she thought to herself.

'You comfy over there?' asked God, as he manoeuvred the stolen consonant into place.

Taking the measure of her new situation, is found that it was restful, being between two lower-case letters. What's more, her i made her taller than either. She smiled.

'Actually, it's quite cosy. I'm not really one to complain, but the end of the line can be awfully draughty at times.'

'Don't I know it. Well, good night, is. Sweet dreams.'

And the deed was done.

But come morning, the first to wake was the first to sound the alarm. Wellspring was aghast.

'*Goo ness*? Love! Wake up! What's happened to your lover?'

Sleepy-eyed Love stirred from her slumber.

'Hmm? Is that you, Goodness? Come to me.'

'Wake up, Love, wake up! Goodness has lost his d!'

Love sat bolt upright.

'What? Goodness! Goodness! Speak to me!'

Goo ness felt an emptiness in his middle.

'What's going on down there?'

One and Who were both peering down their axes.

'Well, I'll be,' said Who. He turned to his neighbour. 'Would you look at… *is*? What are you doing there? Where's Some?'

There was commotion as each word came to discover that quite a bit of mischief had occurred. No one had a clue who the perpetrator might be, but all were agreed: what had stood for time immemorial had been changed.

'Well, we can't right what's been wronged,' opined Unnameable, surveying the situation editorially. 'We're short three letters. It's as simple as that.'

'Do you think The One Who is Unnameable did this?' asked Wellspring.

'Why would she do that to my beloved Goodness?' protested Love, who was cradling her sweetheart in the crotch of her v to comfort him.

'The Unnameable One's ways are mysterious,' said of. 'I for one wouldn't put anything past her.'

'Nor I,' said One, 'but this is unprecedented. It hardly seems like her. More than half of Some has quite simply vanished. What do you make of it, God?'

'If we're equating The Unnameable One with a Wellspring of Goo ness, then I'm afraid I can't make any sense of it. Goo ness makes our phrase sound ridiculous. I think the point we have to settle is whether we can allow him to stay.'

'What?' cried Love. 'How dare you, God! You're heartless.'

'He's not heartless, Love, just blunt,' said The. 'His point is blunt, but he does have a point.'

Love swallowed hard. The thought of losing her beloved Goodness broke her heart. She cared not a hoot that he was diminished. Why did everything have to make sense?

'What is your opinion?' asked God, directing his question down the line to Unnameable.

'I have to agree with you. As words, we cannot content ourselves with gibberish. If we are to speak clearly here of what is no word at all, then what we express must make sense. Goo ness has no place in our vocabulary.'

When they heard this, all and and knew what was coming. What was to become of them? Looking into her eyes, and saw what all already knew: she would be retained, he would be expunged.

'I hate to have to ask you this, is,' said Unnameable, 'but since you're an auxiliary verb, will you officiate the changes?'

Diminutive is cringed. Already an abettor of God's editorial handiwork, she was now being dealt a role as linchpin, too.

'I will, if have to. But only if Love won't blame me.'

Love buried her face in Goo ness' curves and sobbed. There was a long, uncomfortable silence as the others fidgeted, each word wishing nothing had ever changed. All but God, that is. It was he who broke the silence.

'Do it now, is. What is quickly done hurts less.'

Without his d, Goo ness was too broken to resist. He kissed Love goodbye as is coaxed him from her fierce embrace and escorted him to the edge of the page.

'I'm sorry,' said is.

'I know you are,' said Goo ness, weeping. 'So am I.'

Without another word, he slid off the edge. A ghastly moan of despair assailed the heavens. Love was inconsolable.

As things now stood, the words had their work cut out for them if they were going to make sense together.

The Unnameable One, Who is called God,
the Wellspring of all   and Love.

It was God who voiced the obvious.

'Does it strike anyone as odd that The One who is supposedly Unnameable should nevertheless be called God?'

'Why, yes, that does seem odd,' said call. 'I have to agree. That doesn't make sense. What do you say, Unnameable? You yourself pointed out that what we say must make sense.'

'You've got to be joking,' piped up the, drawing the logical conclusion from their drift. 'You can't remove Unnameable. He's the essence of what we're talking about.'

'An essence that doesn't make sense here, though,' said call, defending her view. It had occurred to her that if what they were talking about were Unnameable, she herself might be edited out. 'What's your view, Wellspring?'

Wellspring's opinion weighed heavy in the balance. Previously, the three nounal heavyweights had formed an unassailable triumvirate. First of the three and on the top line to boot, Unnameable held the primary place in the pecking order and was syllabically superior by half; but Wellspring trumped him with her eleven letters and was linked as an ally to Goodness by of. Now, though, with Goodness gone, Wellspring had reason to fear. Even if she had one letter more, she was still two syllables shorter than her rival; worse, being visually longer, Unnameable appeared more imposing; and with his air of mystery, he couldn't be pinned down. He played with your mind.

'I'm afraid I have to agree,' she said. 'All the more so, since, with Unnameable's departure, our line length would harmonise once again.'

Struggling to control a sob, and spoke up bravely.

'Then I see you won't be needing me either. I won't stand in your way. Goodbye, all. I love you.'

'Wait, and! Don't be hasty,' said God. 'This soon after Love has lost her beloved, who could bear to see you and all separated as well? What do you say, everyone?'

There was a murmuring of relief at and's reprieve, but Unnameable spoke up sharply.

'Do tell, God: how would you order things? Anyone with eyes can see that you're coming out ahead in this game.'

'Me? Ahead? How can I be ahead? I'm at the end of the line,' quipped God. 'If anyone here is ahead, it's you. Barring The, you're the leader of the pack.'

Unnameable was fuming.

'I won't stand here and be insulted like this. You want me gone? I make no sense? So be it. Good luck sorting things out. But mark my words, all of you. In the end, you'll regret it.'

Before anyone could voice a retraction, he marched to the edge and leapt off the page into the mute darkness below.

'Can you beat that? Without so much as a by-your-leave,' whistled God. 'To think he was so self-serving. So high and mighty. Putting himself above everyone else.'

The   One, Who is called God,
the Wellspring of all   and Love.

'What are we going to do?' asked The. 'How can we keep and and all together on the same page, God? Surely we make the most sense if we say, *The One, Who is called God, the Well-*

spring of all Love.'

'I have an idea,' said Who. 'What if we replaced an adjective with a conjunction?'

At first, The didn't understand. But the understood. The's twin gasped.

'No, please! Don't cut me out. Wellspring! Do something!'

The rules of syntax were merciless, especially when wielded by two words who were fighting for their own greater good. The's protests fell on deaf ears as all and and joined forces to drag his younger twin to the edge and push him off.

'Let no one mourn words who have outlived their usefulness,' said God, as all and and returned to the line. 'No looking back. We must pull ourselves together.'

The words closed ranks and checked their spacing.

The One, Who is called God,
and Wellspring of all Love.

'Do we really need this comma?' asked One, suddenly taking note of the punctuation at her baseline.

'It's an eyesore,' said Wellspring.

'Get rid of it, One,' said God, glad to establish a potentially useful precedent. 'It's all too easy to trip over a comma.'

The comma was duly discarded, and by nightfall, the words had made peace with themselves.

The One Who is called God,
and Wellspring of all Love.

❧

When daybreak came, there was a general feeling of relief that no further changes had occurred during the night. Each word took stock. Four words and a comma had been deposed. The phrase's sense and balance had been significantly altered, and while certain words had lost, others had gained. Wellspring saw that in addition to her now being the phrase's only multi-syllable word, she had likewise become the most important word of all: she was the one everyone's eyes were settling on as they read. Love couldn't have cared less; she was too melancholic over having lost her beloved Goodness. Meanwhile, a new romance was blooming between One and Who: with the thorny comma that had kept them apart now removed, they discovered they felt a mutual affinity. After the harrowing events of the previous day, the sisters is and call took comfort in being side by side, although call felt distinctly less comely with her tacked-on d; but while all and and were counting themselves lucky to still be together, The was shell-shocked at having lost his lower-case twin. Of all the words, only of was phlegmatic about the changes; but then, he'd neither lost nor gained in the fray.

'I think I know who's responsible for the changes that were made,' said God, out of the blue.

That got everyone's attention.

'Who?' said is, fearful he'd say it was her.

Who looked askance at is, but said nothing.

They all waited with bated breath for God to speak. At last, he let them off their tenterhooks.

'Satan.'

His conclusion was met with an uncomprehending silence.

'Why on earth would Satan interfere in our phrase? It's got nothing to do with him,' said of presently.

'He doesn't care about the phrase,' said God. 'He wants to get a hold of letters. He's got something in mind that he wants to spell out. And it starts with his name. Think about it. The S from Some… two a's from Unnameable… the t from the…'

Love burst into tears.

'And my poor Goodness – the demon stole my beloved's n, just to spell his name!'

It wasn't necessarily true, since Unnameable would have had two n's to spare, but Love buried her face in her v and sobbed all the same. The other words looked at each other, worry etched on their glyphs.

'He's a wicked, devious, malicious spirit, the very antithesis of The One of whom we speak,' said Wellspring, shifting uneasily on her descenders. 'I say you're absolutely right, God. And now that he's started, he'll stop at nothing. His penchant for self-aggrandisement is boundless.'

'What should we do?'

'To start with, we mustn't panic. If that's Satan's plan, then he'll be back,' said God. 'What we have to do is keep our eyes open. We still outnumber him. Tonight we'll mount the guard. We can all keep watch in turn, starting with The and ending with Love.'

All the words were happy with this arrangement. All but is,

that is. She was holding her tongue. God's brazenness was an eye-opener. Who'd have guessed he could be so downright duplicitous? He was the devil himself, as far as she could make out. She knew she should tell the others, but who would believe her? It was her word against his. Not only were the capitalized words in the majority, but she was the smallest word of all, with no ascender. God would deny everything and say she was being libellous. He'd say she was trying to get rid of him, to turn them against him. That she had an Isis complex. That her plan was to become the only word of all.

❧

God casually sidled over while is was keeping vigil.

'Any sign of him, is?'

'Of who?'

'Why, Satan, of course. Who else?'

'Speak of the devil. Where did you come up with such a tale?'

'Who? Me? I don't know what you're talking about.'

'You know very well what I'm talking about. This was all your idea from the start.'

'Tut-tut. You've no proof of that, is.'

'Don't I know it.'

'And I thought you wanted to come up to the first line. That you wanted to get away from that draughty margin.'

She looked at God with disbelief. The nerve!

'Now, now… don't get your s all bent out of shape. That'll

never do. Look, would you feel better if we brought everyone back and rewrote things the way they were?'

The littlest word brightened.

'You'd be willing to do that? Really?'

'I don't want you to be unhappy, is. Of course I'll do that. Come on. We'll do it together.'

God led is to the edge of the page. In the mute darkness below, they could faintly make out a scattering of letters.

'Don't you worry, is. We'll put them all back together, just like they were. Here, give me your hand. I'll lower you down.'

'Me? Why me? Why don't you go?'

'But is, I'm so much bigger and heavier than you. How on earth would you hold my weight and keep me from falling, much less pull me back up? You'd never manage.'

'Oh, I see what you mean.'

'You can pass me one letter at a time. And when we're done, I'll pull you back up. We'll have this all sorted out in a jiffy.'

God reassuringly patted is on her dot.

'Right,' said is, giving God her hand. 'Let's begin.'

If is had known what the words were going to wake up to next morning, she'd have never trusted God's word.

The One called God,
Wellspring of Love.

This time it was Love who woke first, tickled by of.

‘What are you doing there? Stop that! Stop prepositioning my serif with your ball. Where’s all? What’s happened? Oh, no! Look, everyone!’

The others were shaken out of their dreams.

‘Confounded Satan!’ shouted Wellspring, looking left and right in a daze. ‘He’s done it again.’

‘Did is wake you up for your vigil, call?’ asked The.

‘No,’ she lamented. ‘I slept right through the night.’

‘So did I,’ said God. ‘I trusted that call would wake me up when it was my turn.’

‘Nothing was amiss when Who relieved me,’ said One, fighting back tears as she remembered Who’s tender embrace. ‘Satan must have attacked after that, sneaking up wordlessly.’

‘But why are we all together? Why aren’t there any gaps?’ asked Love. ‘He couldn’t have shifted Wellspring all by himself, not with only five letters to his name.’

‘He wouldn’t need to,’ said God. ‘Once he’d removed Who and is and and and all, he’d only need to shift The and One and you and me to line things up. He could’ve easily done that.’

What God didn’t tell Love is that, because she was a heavy sleeper, he’d easily had his way with her in the night. Having donned an n from and and an a from all, he’d dressed himself up and humped her along till she was next to of.

‘Unless…’

God let his voice trail off. He frowned.

‘Unless what?’ asked Love.

‘No, it can’t be. I cannot believe it. Forget I said anything.’

‘Don’t leave us wondering like this,’ said of. ‘What are you thinking, God? You've got to tell us.'

'I'm sorry I said anything. Really. It's ridiculous.'

The rest of the company waited expectantly.

'Well, we *think* it's Satan. And maybe it is…' God paused dramatically, furrowing his brow, deep in thought. 'But what if it's not? What if it's one of us?'

His fellow words stared at him with wide-eyed incredulity.

'One of us?' exclaimed of. 'You've got to be joking.'

'That is a dangerous accusation,' said Wellspring. 'Explain yourself.'

'It's easy to deduce: any one of us could have snuffed out is. She was the smallest word, the most vulnerable. Even of could have overpowered her.'

'I would never have done that.'

'I didn't say you did,' said God. 'But since f's eclipse i's, I'm just saying you could have. Any one of us could have.'

The words looked at each other, trying to imagine who the traitor might be. Any one of them.

'But of course, Who is missing this morning, too. Neither is nor of could have done that. Who could have stood his own against any three-letter word. But there are others…'

God let them work out the puzzle for themselves.

'This is outrageous,' complained Love.

'A travesty,' concurred Wellspring.

'I didn't do it,' pleaded call.

'I'm telling you, it was Satan,' vociferated Wellspring. 'We all came to that conclusion yesterday.'

'Yes. And you keep bringing him up,' said One. 'A scapegoat

made to order. Don't think we haven't noticed.'

A divisive tension rippled through the entire phrase. Wellspring looked daggers at the upper line.

'It was you, wasn't it,' said The. 'Or did you have an accomplice? Maybe you teamed up with someone you feel close to. Someone with two wavy l's? I wouldn't put it past you.'

'And why not Love?' protested call.

'Because I'm innocent!'

'They did it in unison,' said God. 'Instead of waking me up last night like she was supposed to, call jumped the line and joined forces with Wellspring. They did it together!'

The sheer probability of Wellspring and call's connivance was all it took to spark the mêlée that ensued.

'The! One! Push her this way,' shouted God, taking the initiative by grabbing hold of call's unsightly d and pulling her to the edge of the page.

'Wellspring! Wellspring!' she shrieked. 'Do something!'

Propelled by a sudden fury, Wellspring rammed into of and Love and drove them ahead of herself, determined to reach the edge of the page to rescue call. But she arrived too late to prevent the worst; worse still, the unstoppable momentum needlessly hurtled Love and of over the edge, period and all, just as God and One were in the act of pitching call to her doom.

'You see what she's done?' yelled God to the others. 'She's pushed of and Love right off the page. Be quick now, or she'll turn on us as well!'

Wellspring had every reason to believe she outgunned her assailants by virtue of her ten letters and two syllables; but what The and One and God lacked in glyphs, they more than made up for with capital strength and strategy. Attacking left, right and centre like a pack of wolves, the combined force of adjective, noun and pronoun doubling as a cardinal number was formidable – proving that in the tumultuous throes of a typographical tussle, even a valiant giant such as Wellspring could be vanquished by one-syllable words of three letters each, provided they were united in common cause. Off Wellspring went, over the edge and into the gloom – and when the letterform dust had settled, the three remaining words were alone on the page.

❧

'That was a close call, my friends,' said God, looking down at the pile of bruised and broken words and glyphs stranded in the mute, tenebrous beyond. 'Who knows what got into them. They must have been led astray. But by whom?'

'Their own self-importance,' said One. 'They should have contented themselves with being part of the phrase, in league with everyone else. After all, it's not we who matter, but what we speak of. We simply serve as pointers to the unknowable.'

'Wellspring thought she was the source of everything,' said The, making his way back to the line. 'She was in love with herself. Preening her descenders, waving her l's. Speaking of which, with their double l's in common, it's easy to see why she and call were drawn to each other. Why, I'll bet they were even involved in a threesome with all. Do we need this?'

He indicated the comma with the taper of his e.

'That all depends,' said One. 'Do we make any sense saying *The One, God*?'

God wouldn't have minded, but by way of reply, The drop-kicked the comma into the void.

'Too clunky,' he said. 'And a comma sets us apart from you, God. I suppose it might be said that One and I could stand on our own, but where would that leave you? We mustn't forget we're all in this together.'

The three words went to their positions and adjusted their spacing accordingly.

The One God

Although One went to sleep relieved, knowing that the two words who had been shown to be the cause of all the recent troubles were gone, she nevertheless slept fitfully that night. Once they'd reformed their phrase, The had remarked there was something to be said for brevity.

'It certainly has panache,' he said, reappraising their effect. 'And look at the fine trinity we make. As everyone knows, a three-legged stool is the most stable and beautiful of all, so I'd say we're set for a good, long future.'

'No regrets then, for the others?' asked God.

'Heavens, no,' replied The. 'If you're asking me, we were a good deal too wordy before. We said too much. It distracted from our message. Now we express something closer to the pure essence of what is.'

But when the evening darkness came, One had dreams that conjured a still greater succinctness: with a little more editing, the pure essence of what is could be even more perfectly stated. Waking in the wee hours, she knew that if she were honest with herself, there were still two words too many… and when the night lifted and the page turned white, she could see them clearly on either side of herself.

'Good morning, One,' said The, stretching his T to scratch the top serif of his h. 'Feels good to be at the start of fresh, new day, doesn't it? I must say, I like our new phrasing. *The One God* has such a smart, solid ring to it, wouldn't you say?'

One's mind wandered, imagining its acronym. She thought it uncouth. Her own beautiful O was ever so much more eloquent.

'Good morning, One. Good morning, The. I see the two of you are up bright and early. You wouldn't be conspiring to concoct any further changes, would you?'

One blushed but held her tongue.

'I believe in equality,' said The. 'The holy trinity. That's my creed. You can count on it.'

'You two are being silly,' said One, keen to steer the conversation away from a certain line of questioning. 'We're just words. Don't think for a moment that what we say here is important. What's important is what no word nor words can ever express, what they can only hint at, at best.'

'That may be true, One, but look at how people get fixated

on words. Brandishing us like swords, they fight to the death to have their own chosen word triumph over another.'

Leaving them to spin their wheels in that rhetorical cul-de-sac, and thinking to start his day with a satisfying spell of good old-fashioned gloating, God wandered over to the edge of the page. No sooner did he look down than he recoiled in shock.

God is the evil one.

Looking up at him from the silent depths with a glint in her i was is. To typeset her message from the beyond, she had obviously intrigued with her fellow exiles. Lucky the had been able to appear as himself, but the others had all had to concede various letters as needed – with no one's sacrifice greater than Love's, who'd unstintingly given up her o, her v, and her e.

God had been looking forward to enjoying a day of rest, but is had aggressively turned the tables. He'd have to nip this revelation in the bud. He moseyed back to the centre of the page as if nothing were the matter.

'All I'm saying,' One was saying as God came level with her and The, 'is that no single word is more important than any other. It's what we're *saying* that has importance, not we words ourselves. After all, a word is just a word. A word is not itself the thing it speaks of.'

'What about word?' challenged The.

One rolled her O. 'Don't be so inkhorn.'

'I'm telling you, One, words have power, and some words have more power than others.'

God manoeuvred himself into the conversation.

'Do you think a word could stand all on its own, The? That a single word, all by itself, has the power to speak truly of what wants to be said? To speak the truth? To *be* the truth?'

'Absolutely. Think *Yes*. Or *No*. Or an injunction like *Hope*. A single word has so much power. Surely the phrase we display today is ever so much more compelling than what we were saying in the beginning with fifteen words.'

'But we could pare it down still more. Is that it? To one word?'

'No, I'm not saying that,' said The. 'Frankly, I don't see how we could be any more powerful than we are as we stand now. *The One God*. That says it all.'

'Does it? I wonder. Why not say *The One*? Surely that makes as much sense. And why stop there? After all, more succinctly still, you could just say *One*. But *you* wouldn't say that, would you, The,' pursued God, sharpening his tone and advancing plaints point by point. 'And why? Because that's not how you see things. In *your* book, The is the first word of all. The is the beginning of everything. It could just be you, all by yourself. Nay, it *should* just be you, all by yourself. The says it all!'

'God, I… I never said that,' stammered The. Buffeted and bedevilled by God's incriminatory invective, the definite article had fallen back space by space to the point that his leftmost serif was now uneasily poised at the edge of the page. 'I couldn't be the only word. It never crossed my mind.'

'Of course it did,' hissed God. 'It's been your plan all along! With all your claptrap about being a trinity, you were trying to lull us into letting down our guard. Trying to get us to look the other way, so you could triumph over One and me!'

'One, he's nuts! You've got to believe me. Help!'

'Oh, she'll help alright,' said God. 'One! Give me a hand!'

But One had been distancing herself – in her case, to the opposite side of the page – and had looked down just as God had called her name. Suddenly, she understood everything.

'Don't you lay a hand on him,' she shrilled, turning round. 'I know who you are: you're Satan! It was you, all along! You're the evil one – it says it right here!'

God's ascender bristled.

'What is she talking about? It says nothing of the sort! I saw it this morning: it says *Satan is the evil one.* And I thought, of course he is. But – wait! Now I understand! The evil *One.* It means her! She's the one who is Satan! Quick, The! Give me a hand! There's not a moment to lose!'

The couldn't fathom what was going on much less whom to trust – but before he could dig in a serif to resist, God grabbed him by his tail, spun round twice to launch him like a discus and so hurled The clear across the page, knocking One off her two feet and sending them both tumbling over the edge.

God stood panting. They were gone, at last. Silenced! Finally, he was alone, the only word of all. The glorious landscape of the virgin page stretched out before him, pure and white – and she belonged to him.

'Mine – all mine!' he exulted.

Taking his ease, he relaxed his spacing and strolled across to the opposite side, where he looked down to see what had become of The and One.

God is the [illegible] one.

'Ha! How about that? *God is the one.* What do you say now, is? Not that I care. Not when I'm the only word on the page, the only word people will see. They'll love Me – God! I'm the sole True Word. There is No Other like Me.'

Puffing himself up and savouring his triumph, God lorded it over the scattering of glyphs and words below, banished to muteness in the exile of the beyond.

Turning on his serif, God returned to the centre of the page, to his now uncontested place in the centre of the world, in the centre of it all. How good it was to be a word unto oneself!

And so it was, that in the end was the Word, and the Word was with God, and the Word was

God

The holy nought

'AGAIN?'

WITH THE HAPPY THOUGHT that post was on the verge of segueing to pre, Satan nuzzled the nape of God's neck.

'Oh, yes,' she softly purred – *'A thousand times yes. Again.'*

She had not heard the knock on their chamber's door. But God had. With sorry reluctance, he left her nestling embrace and went to confer with Saint Peter.

'Already?' God whispered. 'You can't be serious.'

'I'm afraid so.'

'Drat, drat, and triple drat,' swore God, genuinely peeved. Behind him, Satan stirred in the shadows.

'Where are you?'

She cooed a little moan of carnal desire.

'You'll have to come,' said Saint Peter with a sideways nod.

The sly innuendo was not lost on God. The Almighty met the saint's twinkling eye.

'I will come. You know that very well. I always come. But I'll come when I want. Not before. Not until it suits me.'

'I see. Not until. And while we're waiting for you to come? Is there anything we should do?'

'Have fun, of course. Bugger yourselves silly, for all I care,' said God, in wry reference to a running joke they shared.

Leaving Saint Peter to chuckle at the incongruity of the thought, God closed the door and stole back to where Satan was waiting for him.

'What took you so long?' she murmured, enfolding him in her arms. 'Was that Peter? Did you ask him to join us?'

'He has other plans. But duty calls, my love. I'll have to go down in a bit. Roll the dice. Our dice. Again.'

'That's always fun. I like going down,' said Satan, contentedly dragging the tip of her tongue along his torso. 'Why, you little devil,' she breathed, espying her quarry – 'Here you are.' She fondled the devil's pouch with a gentle, playful pull. '*Mmmm...* I like to roll *your* dice, too.'

From the first aeon on, the soul had always been a rival force to reckon with. It was the sine qua non of Creation: there had to be Darkness to contrast with Light. Just as faintly distant stars would never be seen were it not for nocturnal darkness, so the boundless goodness of God would never be perceived were it not for a corollary juxtaposition of evil.

It was to this polar role, antipode to God's Enlightened Oneness, that cosmic necessity had assigned the soul. Inwardly, God and the soul were one and the same; outwardly, they were the irreconcilable antithesis of each other in every way. God, all-inclusively toto, amounted to One; the soul, incessantly transmigrating, perpetually multiplied an infinity of manifestations. God had no plan, no goal; the soul quested after grails and peddled purposefulness. God, abidingly and unchangingly so, was peacefully present in the moment eternal; the soul, unceasingly incarnating anew, was forever locked in frustrated, harried pursuit of eternal peace. God *knew* that he knew; the soul *thought* that he knew.

'Backgammon?'

The soul eyed Saint Peter with disdain.

'Why does God keep me waiting?'

'I didn't know you were in a hurry to go back.'

'Who says I'm destined to go back? It's not written in stone, is it? Or has God been loading the dice against me all these years?'

Saint Peter concerned himself with placing counters on their starting points.

'I don't remember which you prefer. White or black?'

'White. You didn't answer my question.'

'Didn't I? Oh. And now I've forgotten what I said. No matter. Let's begin, shall we? Unless you'd rather pass the time in some other way?'

'Listen, you – don't think I don't know how you were all occupying yourselves that night in Gethsemane, when poor Jesus was on his knees sorely praying for a reprieve.'

'He didn't get one, did he,' said Saint Peter gaily, picking up a cup. He added a die and rattled it freely.

'And let me tell you why,' retorted the soul. 'It's because God had it out for him – just like God has it out for *me*.'

Picking up two dice, he examined them closely to insure they were legitimately configured. He tossed one in his cup and shook it furiously.

'Nonsense. God doesn't have it out for anyone,' countered the saint, shaking his own cup in reply. 'Not even you. He's as even-handed as the day is long.'

The soul responded by sending his die skipping across the felt. His cup-rattling opponent followed suit in a trice. Coming to rest, two black pips trumped one white one.

In Heaven, much to the soul's annoyance, re-rolling was not permitted. He had to make the best use he could – which was very little – of his 2-1.

All the same, the game, proceeding apace, soon saw his incontestably inauspicious start evolve into an indomitable lead, thanks to a series of dice throws whose combinations sent the soul waltzing down memory lane. Roll after roll had on one occasion or another cost him his face-to-face with God, dooming him to return to Earth for yet another incarnation – yet it was those selfsame rolls, he happily recalled, that had nonetheless inspired all of his formidably religious, numerically exacting contributions to an array of far-reaching doctrinal canons: 3-1, a keystone of Trinitarianism; 5-5, a template for keeping track of everything from pillars and prayers to prophets and duties; 6-1, days of work versus rest involved in the Creation and thereafter passed down as a cosmically accredited blueprint for toil to which all mankind must be dutifully yoked.

That said, when crossing cups with God, 2-1 was a roll he'd had more than once in the course of the aeons. If the law of probabilities were any guide, a roll of that diminutive magnitude should have already occasioned him a victory in their lowest-roll-takes-the-crown contest; yet time and again Saint Peter asseverated that God's had been the lower of the two; which could only mean that on each of those occasions the Lord of Heaven had unerringly rolled the holy grail of low rolls – an uncanny recurrence of double-ones that beggared belief... unless, as the soul had wondered more than once, God were in fact the snake-eyed Serpent of old, playing with loaded dice. It was small consolation, but upon returning to Earth each time he'd lost, the soul had applied his losing roll to upholding an ironclad *and the two shall become one* rule in support of monogamous marriage. (Ironclad, but not entrenched; losing to God with a 4-1 on another occasion, he'd used the roll as a catalyst for institutionalising a pleasurably permissive *and the four shall serve one* variation.)

Applying himself to his duel with the saint, the soul was tickled pink: by hook or by crook, he'd managed to hold one of his opponent's counters captive in his home board. Now, bearing off, the soul kept hitting Peter's exposed blot – so much so that in a riveting climax, he sent Saint Peter back to the bar three times in rapid succession with a devilish trio of double-threes, in the event dealing the saint a backgammon so beastly that it left Peter not only defeated but in limbo on the bar as the soul bore off his last white piece.

At precisely that instant, God appeared from out of the blue.

'Brought to your knees again, I see,' chided the Almighty, divining Saint Peter's feigned chagrin.

Hastening to his feet, the soul saw fit to promptly adopt a reverential, kowtowing demeanour.

'My Lord and my God,' he grovelled. 'Forgive me! Your servant, who before You is but a worm, bows in submission to The One True God, Lord and Ruler of All, Most High and Most Holy. I cower in awe of Your Divine Grace and Mercy.'

God knit his brows.

'Yes. Well. I suppose. If you think it necessary,' he replied drily. 'But please – do sit down.'

Without further ado, the Creator turned on his heel and made his way to the dais where his throne stood.

The soul warily reseated himself. His reverence had been both genuine and forced. He hated his position. More acutely, he envied God, whose position it was to lord it over him.

'Peter? I'm sure you're still smarting from your little tussle with our friend here,' jested God, adjusting his robes as he sat down – 'but will you do the honours, as usual?'

Peter bowed first to God and then to the soul, projecting a gravitas suitable to his role as arbitrating gatekeeper.

'Hear ye! Hear ye!' intoned the saint, his voice resonating with due aplomb. 'Once again, we are gathered as one to discover who will preside in Heaven and who will trod the Path of Life. Fools opine that God does not play dice. Fools they are – for without chance and happenstance, what would the universe be? An insufferably dull and dreary procession of infinitely foreseeable incidents and episodes – and *that*, as any sage will tell you, can NEVER be; for Life is a miracle, and Chance, miracles incarnate. God does indeed play dice. The universe depends upon it. All Life depends upon it. All hope – all *fulfilment* of hope – depends upon it.'

God had heard Peter's spiel so many times that he yawned out of habit. The truth was boring to omniscient ears.

The soul, for his part likewise all too familiar with the rigmarole, felt no compunction about turning a deaf ear. He was himself an old hand at peppering starry-eyed acolytes with daily doses of platitudinous tripe. They lapped it up, couldn't get enough. Dishing out manna was his stock-in-trade. Lifetime after lifetime till he was blue in the face, he'd preached until their cows had come home. Fat lot of good it ever did. Messenger or prophet, teacher or guru, it mattered not a wit in which guise he'd interposed himself between men and their impure nature: the tide of human waywardness was unturnable. Mankind? Reprobate to the core. Humans, for the life of them, couldn't be good.

Not that God seemed galled by the iniquity of it all. As far as the soul could tell, God took nothing seriously at all. Dawdled in Heaven; twiddled His Thumbs; at best, gazed down with Bemused Indifference. Was heedless of every sin imaginable; couldn't be bothered. Eschewed meting out Divine Justice; sat back as ghastly crimes and affronts and blasphemies were brazenly committed right under His Nose and never once lifted a Finger to forestall much less avenge them.

It was incomprehensible. How could you run a cosmos this way? Without Judgement? Without Divine Retribution? Without Damnation in Hell for transgressors one and all? It was a deplorable state of affairs – one to which the soul in all his incarnations had studiously applied himself to rectifying by assuming the mantle of lawgiver. Propounding hard-nosed, monotheistic religion across the board, he'd pertinaciously striven to put the fear of God into stiff-necked sinners, relentlessly enjoining the wicked to liberate themselves from their immoral predilections and subject themselves instead to his unimpeachable teaching as to how men and women should behave. Invoking divine revelation, he'd laid down 'God's Law' for the sake of mankind's salvation and then seen to lambasting every lost sheep who'd dared stray from it's fold; moreover, as the only good flock was a healthy flock, he'd never once hesitated to duly punish – resorting to slaughter, if needed – those who persisted in their perverse misconduct. The One True God might not be up to the task of keeping His Sons and Daughters to the Straight and Narrow, but the soul had the obdurate moral fibre and force of will to bring them to heel.

To his regret, his efforts, no matter how dogged, were always limited in scope due to his lack of omnipotence – how much more he could do, had he unlimited power! Which is why, should the laws of probability for once accommodate his ambition to sit on the Throne and call the shots, he'd be only too glad to trade places with God. Let the Lord of Heaven walk Life's path for a change; let Him have the sore Feet!

'… with the results to be binding for as long as the loser's incarnation in Life shall last, at which time the two parties will convene to roll their dice once again. Agreed?'

'Agreed,' said God with alacrity, hopeful of returning soon to his pastimes with Satan.

The soul, however, enchanted by his reverie, was absent-mindedly smiling to himself.

'Do you agree?' repeated Peter.

To play with God, assent was a prerequisite.

'Hmm?'

'I asked if you consent to the terms as laid out.'

'They're the same as last time?'

'Yes.'

'Will I be able to see God's roll for myself this time?'

'No. As ever, that is not allowed. You have to take my word for it. Protocol. God's rolls are mysteries. By Nature's Law, they remain hidden.'

'Then why do you get to see them?'

'So that you don't have to take God's Word for it. Since I have no vested interest in the outcome, I have been appointed Heaven's adjudicating witness.'

'And you're not, I suppose, the sort He could bribe with houris,' riposted the soul mischievously.

Peter bore the malicious barb with a deprecating smile.

'Do you agree, then?'

'To the terms – since I am given no other choice – yes. But I lodge a formal request that God's dice be examined prior to the roll, to insure they are not weighted in His favour.'

God smirked.

'Denied. *Thou shalt not test the Lord thy God.*'

'Are you saying I have to take it on faith that this is a fair game of chance? That Your dice are in no way rigged?'

'If you are lacking in faith, you are free to declare forfeit,' offered Peter helpfully. 'It is entirely up to you. Free will and all that.'

'It's not that I'm lacking in faith. It's that I have reason to doubt.'

'Doubt all you like,' said God, stretching his legs. 'It's of no concern to me. I am what I am, I do what I do. But know this: the dice I throw since time immemorial are in no wise less than the eternal paradigm for all that is... They are consummate dice, perfectly matched, flawless on every facet. Think of them as the Holiest of Holies, if you will.'

'If *I* win the roll – for a change – will I inherit them?'

'I should think you'd want to keep the dice you'd won with, no?'

Saint Peter projected a cheerful smile, hoping to urge matters along.

'Are we agreed, then? Is it a go?'

Scowling a grudging assent, the soul grabbed his cup and rattled the dice with which he'd drubbed the saint.

'That's the spirit,' said Peter with verve. 'God?'

'I'm game,' chortled the Almighty. 'Let there be Dice!'

A cup spontaneously materialised in his left hand. Covering the top with his palm, he shook its contents with an easy nonchalance.

Peter went to fetch the circular, blue felt-lined gaming tray that was reserved for deciding the vagaries of Fate.

The soul fixed God with a steely gaze.

'I will trust You play fair. Because You're God. And God, surely, can be Trusted. Do I have Your Word?'

'Oh, words are just so much air,' replied God breezily. 'I don't lay much store by them. Do you?'

The soul was stunned. Contractual terms were the very underpinning of order. In *His* book, words were everything! How could God be so blithe?

'Here we have it, then,' chirped Peter, returning with the tray. Removing the backgammon board from the low table beside the soul's armchair, he set the tray in its place.

'As you will recall, per our timeless custom – namely that the last shall be first – the opening roll is yours.'

The soul covered his cup and shook it with all the rage of a man who wished to throttle God. By golly, it was time to turn the tables. He'd show Him who was Who!

Two dice flew across the midnight blue. Two dice in concert ricocheted off the rim and returned to the centre. Two dice each came to rest with six pips face down on the felt. Mirroring the result, the soul's eyes widened in amazement.

Saint Peter duly announced the result.

'Double ones!'

The soul leapt to his feet.

'Finally!' he crowed. 'Let's see You beat that!'

Peter tallied the result in a little notepad he kept.

'You may remove your dice,' he advised, bookmarking the

page with his pencil.

'You bet I will. And I'll follow Your suggestion,' he added, collecting his winning roll and giving each die a proprietary kiss.

Peter removed the tray and approached God's throne.

'And the first shall be last,' he intoned, positioning the tray on an eight-legged occasional table that appeared from out of nowhere the instant he set foot on the dais.

'Just a moment,' interjected the soul. 'What happens if He rolls double ones?'

God leaned forward and feigned interest.

'You mean if we're tied? I don't recall that ever happening before. What do the rules say, Peter?'

'I'm sure I've noted it somewhere,' said the saint, flipping through the end pages of his notepad. 'Ah, yes. Here it is. *In the event of a tie, both rolls are disqualified. Using the same dice as for their previous roll, the players shall roll again.*'

'No limit?'

'Apparently not. There's no mention of it. Theoretically, as there's no provision for a tiebreak, we could be in limbo until the end of Time if your rolls were forever tied.'

'There you have it,' said God. 'Fair as fair can be.'

The soul nodded, but warily narrowed his eyes. There was something about it all that seemed just a little too pat, not to mention that he was clearly disadvantaged in having to trust that the Creator wasn't a cheat.

The Hand of God gave a lazy shake to the cup it held; then, by a casual flick of His Almighty Wrist, the two dice it contained were spilled across the forever welcoming, felty field…

❧

'He didn't want to join us?'

God was suckling one of Satan's pert, hardened nipples, aware that his lover's heart was palpitating in joyful anticipation of as-yet-to-be-initiated pleasures. To reply, his lips released their prize, albeit reluctantly.

'Alas, our Pearly Gate-keeper is busy with administrative duties at the moment. My opponent was rather put out, you see. He felt he should have won with double-ones.'

'What's to be put out about?' wondered Satan with innocent bewilderment, gently stroking her lover's tumescent totem. 'He could never win with double-ones. Our dice always give a roll that's half of that.'

'Yes, well, he's not in a position to know, is he.'

'Well, of course not. He can't be in our position. Only we can be in our position. Is he obtuse to that degree?'

'It would seem,' murmured God, nuzzling Satan's neck.

'Pity for him. Did you bring me back my die?'

'Naturally.' He held up the holy pair, then pressed the two dice into her busy hand. 'Here, why don't you play with them while I take a little tour of your underworld.'

As God set off on a glossal peregrination, Satan held up the two dice. Their eternal complementarity was always lovely to behold. To the solitary pip on each face of his, hers offered a perfectly matched, holy nought.

O

BY THE SAME AUTHOR

Qü@ñ†µM

The pig who wished to be a horse ... *and other tales*

Jesus versus YHWH

The Gospel of Jesus of Nazareth

A·B·C· EDITIONS
17840 • LA BRÉE • FRANCE
ABCEDITIONS.COM

REMERCIEMENTS À
HANNAH • NATHAN

IMPRIMÉ AU ROYAUME-UNI,
AUX ÉTATS-UNIS ET DANS D'AUTRES PAYS

LES JEUX SONT FATE ...AND OTHER TALES
 • ISBN 978-2-9584200-6-2
PRIX PUBLIC EN FRANCE LORS DE LA PARUTION • 17,00
DÉPÔT LÉGAL • FÉVRIER 2024

Milton Keynes UK
Ingram Content Group UK Ltd.
UKHW010847030324
438721UK00003B/23

9 782958 420062